Tea £2
51

Luisa Plaja lives in Devon with her husband and two young children. She is a huge fan of teenage chick-lit and loves reading, writing and pretending she can do things she can't, like ice skating and telling jokes.

Praise for her books:

'A cute, sweet and funny read.'
Meg Cabot, on *Split by a Kiss*

It's rare to find a book like this – that has a brand new, never-told-before story, brilliant writing, lots of very realistic scenarios and some hilarious characters. It really is the ultimate in teen fiction.'
Bookbag, on *Split by a Kiss*

'A great, quick, light, fun read . . . I loved it!'
Once Upon a Bookcase, on *Swapped by a Kiss*

'Original and true to life, and sure to appeal to a wide range of readers . . . You will thoroughly enjoy this teen tale of extremes.'
Wondrous Reads, on *Extreme Kissing*

www
D1152137

Also by Luisa Plaja:

Split by a Kiss
Swapped by a Kiss
Extreme Kissing

kiss date love hate

Luisa Plaja

CORGI BOOKS

KISS DATE LOVE HATE

A CORGI BOOK 978 0 552 56097 9

Published in Great Britain by Corgi Books,
an imprint of Random House Children's Books
A Random House Group Company

This edition published 2011

3 5 7 9 10 8 6 4 2

Copyright © Luisa Plaja, 2011

The right of Luisa Plaja to be identified as the author of this work has been
asserted in accordance with the Copyright, Designs and Patents Act 1988.

All rights reserved. No part of this publication may be reproduced,
stored in a retrieval system, or transmitted in any form or by any
means, electronic, mechanical, photocopying, recording or
otherwise, without the prior permission of the publishers.

The Random House Group Limited supports The Forest Stewardship
Council (FSC®), the leading international forest certification organisation.
Our books carrying the FSC label are printed on FSC® certified paper.
FSC is the only forest certification scheme endorsed by the leading
environmental organisations, including Greenpeace. Our
paper procurement policy can be found at
www.randomhouse.co.uk/environment

Set in 11/17pt Palatino by
Falcon Oast Graphic Art Ltd.

Corgi Books are published by Random House Children's Books,
61–63 Uxbridge Road, London W5 5SA

www.kidsatrandomhouse.co.uk
www.totallyrandombooks.co.uk
www.randomhouse.co.uk

Addresses for companies within The Random House Group Limited can be
found at: www.randomhouse.co.uk/offices.htm

THE RANDOM HOUSE GROUP Limited Reg. No. 954009

A CIP catalogue record for this book is available from the British Library.

Printed and bound in Great Britain by Clays Ltd, St Ives PLC

To Isabella and Rocco

Special thanks to Lauren Buckland and Jodie Marsh for all their help; Debs Riccio, Tina Thompson and Kate Bubb for answering technical questions; Susie Day, Emily Gale, Caroline Green, Alexandra Fouracres, Tabitha Reed, Keris Stainton and all my writing, tweeting and book-blogging friends for their support; and Blind Ditch and the VANLAND team for giving me the film-making bug.

In memory of Rosemary Canter

PART ONE:

kiss

It's just another lunch time on the Chairs of Doom outside Mr Trench's office. I'm sort of a permanent fixture here. If the chairs weren't so wobbly, I'd probably have grown roots by now. Maybe when I finally leave school, once I've scraped GCSEs and limped through enough sixth form to make Mum (and my boffin friend Jess) happy, they'll put a plaque against the exposed bricks where my head is resting now.

Lex Murphy woz ere! it'll say. Or the posh, plaque-friendly equivalent: *Alexa No-Middle-Name Murphy frequented this hallowed spot. Many a luncheon time she awaited here for Sir Trench of Foot to deliver another Life-changing Speech before she was free to find Jess at their usual bench by Ye Olde Vending Machine. And Jess had better not be talking to Gemma the Evil when Lex gets there or else . . . Lex will pretend everything's fine, as usual.*

Anyway, it's no big deal. That I'm here, I mean. That Jess still talks to Gemma is a pain, but I don't really want

3

them to know that I care, so I kind of put up with it. They don't see each other much these days anyway. Our old loose group of friends-forever has pretty much disbanded lately. The boys are all in the sixth form now, and they've left me, Jess and Gemma behind, but that's not the only reason we've drifted apart. Jess is far too wrapped up in being a perfect pre-GCSE student, and Gemma is far too wrapped around Matt. *My* Matt. The exact same Matt that *she* told me wasn't right for me.

She swears she didn't plan on getting together with him after we broke up, but that's exactly what happened, so she can swear all she likes. Gemma Grant might still officially be my friend, as far as the outside world can see, but I know the truth. She is evil. Getting into trouble in geography over my attitude to Gemma is totally worth another lunch time outside Mr Trench's office.

I know the routine by now. In a few minutes the Trenchmeister will call me in and I'll get a big dose of Trench-like disappointment, some shaking of the Trench Head, and a few minutes of Trench Speech. Trenchie recites this speech from a script he memorized about a million years ago, and he barely even pauses while he's delivering it. He booms on about RESPECT-ING MY PEERS and RESPECTING MY SCHOOL and how this equals RESPECTING MYSELF, though really I don't see how what I called Gemma earlier could have anything to do with the way I look after myself. (I do *that* very well, really, apart from the Great Home Hair Extension Disaster of last week. But I think the clumpy bald bit on top of my head might get me the sympathy vote with Trenchie and shorten today's lecture by several booms. It's an unexpected win.)

Spending part of lunch break here on a regular basis is getting a bit boring, though. I'm so glad it's nearly half term. There's not much to see at the dead end of the darkest corridor, right by the posh main entrance that we're never supposed to use unless we've had a doctor's appointment or something and we're supremely, legitimately late and have to sign in. You can't even watch the school go by from here because no one who isn't part of the species named 'Teacher' is allowed to enter the Corridor of Power. Oh, unless you're part of the species nicknamed 'Improver' and you're here for a lecture, of course.

'Improvers' are students who are either: 1) generally a bit rubbish at keeping out of trouble, 2) never actually at school, or 3) totally brainless. I seem to have been an Improver for ever, and quite honestly I think it's a bit late for me now. Chances are I'm never actually going to 'improve'. Mr Trench can try out his theories all he likes, but I seem to be firmly dis-en-Trenched. I am a *disprover*. I mostly only turn up at school to make Mum happy, and because if I wasn't here I'd have no one to hang around with, which would be even more boring than school. I spend enough time in my own world as it is.

I shift in my chair and it squeaks horribly in protest, but it's not as bad as the chair next to it, which I know from last week is in danger of terminal collapse. I'm busy pondering whether I should bring my own non-broken chair to school, just for the purposes of sitting here – I could get one of those folding canvas ones that people take to music festivals, with a little net drinks holder in the arm – when a boy lands in the broken Chair of Doom next to me.

'If I were you,' I say helpfully, 'I wouldn't sit— Oh.'

There's a crash, and then he's in a heap on the floor, long limbs sprawling, which means I get to sneakily check him out for the two seconds before he picks himself up.

Because he's not just *any* boy. He's Drew Ashton, Jess's wicked Scottish step-cousin, who was sent to live with Jess's family at the start of this term. He's just about the only boy in the school who doesn't know the entire *Who's Who* of past dating and dumping dramas between our friends. This makes spending time with him absolutely refreshing. He's like a clean slate.

He's also a total bad boy. The official story is that he's here because he had nowhere else to live – his dad got some foreign work placement and took his mum and little brothers and sisters along, but because of something to do with exams, Drew stayed in Scotland with his nan. Then, in the summer, his nan died, and Drew moved in with his nearest relative, Jess's stepdad.

The unofficial story, though – the one I've made up with the help of bits and pieces that Jess tries not to tell me – is that Drew has been sent to live with the Hartfords because his parents hope she'll be a good influence on him. I reckon Drew's mum looked at her little brother's new wife, noticed the perfection of his new step-child (Jess) and thought, *Right, well, your woman can sort out* this *one too.*

Drew could never be anything like Jess, though. Jess is glossy and groomed and studious, and Drew is . . . well, the total opposite. You can tell instantly by his hair and his stubble and his eyebrow piercing. (He's Year Twelve, so he gets to wear what he likes. And, wow, I like what he wears.) You can also tell by the way he walks, like he has no respect for anyone, let alone the inhabitants of the Corridor of Power. He's in the same year as all my other male friends, but he is nothing like any of them. He doesn't play football like Matt and Hayden and Cam, and he doesn't hang around the library like George. In fact, I almost never see him at school at all, except outside Mr Trench's office, like today.

Drew is clearly a Type Two Improver, or 'Non-Attender', as Mr Trench sometimes calls the guys who spend school hours down the arcade. They get pulled into his office the minute they show their faces at school. (No wonder they rarely turn up. Teachers really need to think that one through.) It's not so bad when you're a sixth-former and you're actually allowed to escape sometimes, but if you miss certain parts of the school day, then it's still frowned on, and Mr Trench does love a good frown.

Oops, I've been staring at Drew for ages. He's put the broken chair back, ready for someone else to sit on – that's the kind of rebel he is – and he's staring right back at me. Correction: he's staring at the signs of hair-extension disaster on top of my head.

'You OK?' he asks me.

I think he means the bald patch but I choose to ignore it. I pull at my hair and make sure my ears are covered. 'You're the one who just got friendly with the ground,' I remind him. 'Are *you* OK?'

He brushes himself off, shrugs a bit and grins at me. Then he tells me that he's most displeased that he has to visit Mr Trench today. Course, he says it a whole lot ruder than that, and it makes a passing teacher glare at us and tut. We catch each other's eye after that and stifle laughs.

Drew might be the opposite of Jess but he's also so far away in personality from someone like Matt that sometimes I'm amazed I like him so much. Not that Matt doesn't swear, but he sort of restricts it to his male friends, and I think he, Cam and Hayden would die if they thought a teacher had overheard them. Plus those boys are generally a bit rubbish at talking to girls. Gemma and I have both been out with Cam and Hayden, but back when we were so young that it was all about holding hands for five minutes and then dumping them. (And actually, I think I dated and dumped them both before she did.) Matt was different. Matt was this year and Matt broke my heart, even if all my friends think it was the other way round.

Except Gemma, of course. And she seems to have brought out a side of Matt that I never knew existed. He's turned into a devoted boyfriend-type, glued to Gemma's side. I have no idea what they talk about.

Drew, on the other hand, is a total free spirit. He doesn't really hang around with anyone, or go out with anyone, and it's such a contrast to my usual crowd. It's always a highlight for me when he joins me in the Corridor of Power. He has these amazingly expressive eyebrows, and we've had some good chats out here about nothing much – mostly stuff that Drew remembers about going to Jess's mum's wedding to his uncle four years ago. He actually met me that day – I was giggling with Gemma for most of the time, on a bit of a sugar high – but I don't think he remembers me and my eleven-year-old dorkiness, which is probably a good thing. He remembers lots of other people, though, and we've had laughs about Jess's mad extended family, which is now even more extended and even madder – except for the fact that it includes supercool Drew.

Today he doesn't mention Jess or her family. He just waggles those eyebrows, gives me another grin and asks, 'So what are you in for this time? Been giving poisoned apples to teachers again?'

I made that up a couple of weeks ago when he asked me why I was here. I like thinking up ridiculous crimes that make Drew laugh. But today his eyebrows have made my mind go blank, so I opt for the boring truth.

'I had a fight with another girl in the middle of geography.'

The eyebrows display intrigue. 'A punch-up or a wee bit of verbal?'

I love the way the words curl round his mouth. I mentioned this casually to Jess once and she said it's just the way all Scottish people talk, but I'm not so sure. I think Drew has really interesting lips. I also love the way he doesn't say 'Mee-OW!' or make sexist comments about cat-fights, or do anything remotely feline at all. Normal boys would totally get their cat on, given a chance like this. They did it in geography earlier, which is why Ms Cosgrove called me 'disruptive'. It's so unfair. That lot should be in trouble, not me. My remark was private, and I didn't even think it was all that loud, not until the mewing boys broadcast it. Ms Cosgrove, our Geography teacher, is supposed to be a feminist. She should know better than to blame a *girl*, even if I might technically have started it.

'Just words . . .' I think about it. 'Unfortunately.' It's sometimes tempting, but I could never do anything physically violent.

Drew nods seriously. He probably *would* – goes with the bad-boy territory. There are rumours that he has a string of ASBOs and everything, even though Jess claims that's not true. 'He *wishes*,' she says, allowing herself a good eye-roll.

Drew balances himself on the slightly-less-broken Chair of Doom on the other side of me. 'Well, I bet she deserved it,' he says. He looks at me expectantly.

'Gemma definitely deserved it,' I reply. I don't want to tell him why. I mean, I suppose Jess might talk about her friends at home, so he could have heard things about Gemma. He might even know that Gemma's boyfriend is my ex. But Jess says she barely sees 'that delinquent' – i.e. Drew – so probably not.

His eyebrows definitely say: *Tell me more*.

I'm not exactly sure why I don't want to tell him. Maybe it would feel weird to talk about my ex-boyfriend, and how miffed I am (to put it mildly) that Gemma is going out with him. But *why* would it feel weird? It's true that I'm trying to keep these feelings a

11

secret from my friends, because our group's falling apart enough as it is. But Drew barely talks to any of them – not even his cousin Jess. (Or *especially* not his cousin Jess.)

And it can't be because I fancy Drew. Because I don't – not really. He's not like Matt. I appreciate Drew's gorgeousness and the lovely way he talks to me, but as a distant bystander, you know. The way people admire pictures of fit filmstars at premieres. I don't go hot and cold when I see him, like I do when I see Matt. Matt's always surrounded by people (and now by Gemma), always the centre of attention. He's Mr Popular, everyone's friend. Drew's always on his own, if he's here at all. I think most people are a bit scared of him.

I'm not scared of Drew, but maybe I'm a bit freaked out by the way he doesn't seem to care what anyone thinks of him.

One thing's for sure: Drew is not Matt.

Drew's still waiting for me to reply, his long legs stretched out in front of him. He tips his head back so that I can't see his gorgeous mouth any more, but I can see his body leaning dangerously back in the rickety chair with his arms behind his head. I wonder if he knows how hot that makes him look.

The way a film star on a red carpet might look hot, I mean. From a distance.

Drew straightens up, looking right at me. 'I said,

what did she do?' He doesn't seem annoyed that I totally missed his question because I was gazing at his body. (Though he can't have known that's what I was doing. I hope.)

I don't have to think of a suitable reply because the door beside us opens and Mr Trench appears in all his tweedy, teacherly glory.

'Andrew Ashton and Alexa Murphy!' he blares, even though we're the only people here and there is seriously no need. No one in the world could have any trouble catching Mr Trench's words. 'Step this way, please!'

'Both of us?' I ask, startled, not looking at Drew. 'Together?'

'Yes. Together. Come ON, I haven't got all DAY!' Mr Trench booms. 'I'm asking you to step into my office, not hold hands and dance a jig!'

'Shame,' I think Drew mumbles as we walk in, which gives me a delicious kind of feeling that I like slightly too much, considering.

Though he probably means it's a shame he has to spend his lunch break going into Trenchie's den with his step-cousin's dorky mate. Or maybe he's secretly into dancing jigs.

So we go in and, within minutes, Trenchie has boomed his ultra-cruel and unusual punishment at us.

And it is the *worst* idea ever.

13

'It is the *best* idea ever!' George enthuses a few hours later, going so far as to drop his Nintendo DS on his *Lord of the Rings* duvet cover in excitement.

George Richards is probably the main boy in my life right now, if you can call him a boy. I mean, he's definitely male, and he's in the year above me at school, so still technically a 'boy', possibly even bordering on a 'man'. But he's not like a proper boy (or borderline man). He's not the kind you can lust after. He's a friend. In fact, he's probably my *best* friend right now, what with Jess being in love with her schoolwork and Gemma being in love with my Matt.

George's status as my best friend is a bit worrying, though, for a couple of reasons. The biggest one is that his dad and my mum went out together for a while when we were younger. They fell out big-time, and now my mum assures me that their relationship is 'civilized' and they can 'converse like adults'. But I haven't seen any evidence of it myself, and anyway I'm not sure I've ever heard Mum converse with anybody like an adult. She's a nurse and she treats everyone the same – like a slightly exasperating patient who needs sorting out as quickly and efficiently as possible. She especially does that with me, even now, four years after I had my big scary brush with an illness called meningitis. I ended up in hospital for a while, and since then I sometimes think she actually does see me as a patient and not her daughter.

Anyway, George and his dad moved in next door a few years before all that. George's dad met my mum and they bonded over tea, biscuits and a love of moaning about single parenthood. For a while George's dad and my mum became sort-of-a-couple. Now, of course, they are very-much-not-a-couple. This means that George and I were briefly sort-of-brother-and-sister, and now we probably shouldn't get on any more, out of loyalty to our parents. But we do, and it can be awkward, especially because George and his dad live so close, and Mum doesn't exactly approve of me spending time with them. I've learned an important life lesson out of this: don't ever go out with anyone you can't escape from easily when it all goes wrong. This also applies to seeing people from school, obviously: e.g. Matt. Ouch.

Jess would never, ever date anyone from school, not if he was the last guy on earth – not because of the potential post-breakup trauma, but because she says all the boys at school, even the ones in the sixth form, are 'incredibly immature'. She's not completely wrong about that, but still. This is Worry Number Two: George is madly in love with Jess, and has been for years. So the guy who's now probably my best friend (George) fancies the girl who all the world thinks is my best friend (Jess), who would never look twice at him in a

15

million years. I can't pretend this is not occasionally a problem.

The final reason it's worrying that George is my best friend is because he's, well, a really strange person. And I mean that kindly, I swear. I love him like a brother. But like a slightly embarrassing brother that you might take a few steps away from and cringe a bit if someone really cool saw you together in public.

Basically, apart from his fascination with computer games and consoles, and his love of films about elves and orcs, George was born into the wrong era. I think he would be the first to agree with this statement, so I'm not being mean. He dresses like some kind of Victorian gentleman – all proper trousers and ironed shirts and blazers and stuff – and he talks like an old person. This isn't so bad at school, although George always looks like he's still wearing uniform despite being in the sixth form, and he's a bit too polite to teachers. But he looks and talks the same on Saturdays and Sundays, which is unlikely to attract Jess. Or any girl, ever.

'I'm delighted that you'll be on the same course as me and Jess,' he says in his proper way, which is so far from cool that it practically sizzles.

I give him a stern look. 'You make it sound like you and Jess are going *together*.'

'In my dreams,' George sighs. 'In my dreams, Lex, we are.'

I really don't want to know about George's dreams. 'Anyway, I haven't agreed to go yet,' I tell him. I explain that Mr Trench suggested the Digital Media (aka film-making) course as a punishment. Though Trenchie called it an 'opportunity' and went on and on about the 'level playing field of the visual arts' and how it would present 'the right kind of environment for students like you two' – meaning me and Drew. Apparently it would 'enable' us, and help us to 'fulfil our potential'. Or something. So much for Trenchie insisting that the school didn't believe in giving any student 'special treatment', which is what he told my mum when I came back to school after my meningitis scare and I'd missed a ton of school stuff that I've never really caught up on. My regular meetings with Mr Trench seem pretty *special*, even though the word that gets used in our school, at least at my age, is 'transitional'.

Anyway, whichever way Trencharoony dresses it up, it's obvious that he's really giving me an elaborate form of detention, seeing as it will rob me of my entire half-term holiday and deprive me of any chance of a lie-in for five whole days. I think it has to be a government bid to keep Improvers off the streets, as Mr Trench went on and on about how perfect it was for me and Drew. Then he told us to 'strongly consider it', in a tone of voice that suggested we had no choice. But I bet Drew won't turn up. It's essentially just another thing for a Non-Attender not to attend.

George is looking at me, all shocked.

'Yeah, I probably won't go.' I enjoy forming those words.

'But . . .' George never understands how I can get into trouble at school. He has never been told off in his life. Come to think of it, that's one thing he actually has in common with Jess. 'But, Lex, doesn't Mr Trench mean that you *have* to go?'

Yes, probably. 'No. I think he just needs to tell the local authority he's made an effort to get some Improvers on the course to balance out the boffins like you and Jess.'

'Jess is very intelligent,' George says dreamily. 'And beautiful too.' He snaps out of it and adds quickly, 'And so are you, Lex.'

I roll my eyes. Jess is the main reason George is on the course, even though he does love film. He loves Jess more, though. She was the first person to sign up, because she goes to a Gifted and Talented group run by Mr Trench, and apparently he told her that a course like that would help her 'look well-rounded' on her CV and she could 'still do GCSE work in the evenings'. She's forever quoting Mr Trench as if he's some kind of celebrity life coach instead of just an extremely annoying teacher. And ever since the start of this school year, Jess has been totally single-minded about her Future with a capital F. She even gave up her dance classes, which used to be her favourite thing in the world, because she said the after-school lessons clashed with her homework schedule, and Lady Gaga routines weren't really helpful for her Future. I don't really understand Jess any more.

Then Matt signed up for the film course because it's what he does – he's always been a total joiner. This meant Cam and Hayden signed up too, because they're Matt's sidekicks, and Gemma had to follow, because she can't take a breath without Matt these days. After that, I had no choice, even though out of all our gang I'm probably the most interested in film. There is no way I could stand a week of Matt and Gemma all over each other.

Not that any of my friends will even miss me.

'It would be wonderful to have you there,' George says.

Except faithful George.

'In a different environment like that, it could be my chance with Jess,' he adds. 'You can put in a good word for me.'

Not necessarily faithful to *me*, though. 'I've put in thousands of excellent words for you ever since we were six and you made me propose to her for you with that ready-salted Hula Hoop ring,' I remind him.

'It was cheese and onion,' he corrects me wistfully. 'And I still can't believe she jilted me at the playground altar. She'll learn the error of her ways, though, sooner or later—'

19

Or never. 'George, listen, I'm not doing it. I'm not wasting my half-term cooped up in a classroom with Mr Trench, with you mooning over Jess.' *And with Gemma drooling over Matt*, I don't add.

'It won't be a waste! It'll be excellent! You know you'll love it. It's so *you*!'

My mobile does a wild vibration dance from somewhere inside my school bag and I reach in to extract it. I came straight here after school, like I usually do when Mum is on lates at work. George's dad, Martin, works from home on some computer thing and he doesn't often surface from his basement office. When he does, he's usually quite nice to me, despite the fact that he and my mum aren't exactly speaking. Martin is OK, really, for a dumped almost-stepdad.

I press buttons on my phone while George keeps wheedling. I look at him as he says, 'Promise me you'll go, O great Ah-LEX-ah, O Gracious One, O wondrous patchy-headed beauty and person who *isn't* rude for reading text messages while I'm talking to you . . ..'

I turn back to the message. It's from Jess. It says: Drew def on film course! Disaster!

With George definitely still pleading in the background, I text back: No way will he turn up! I talked about this with Jess earlier. She agreed that Drew wouldn't go, and she sounded pretty relieved about it too.

20

She replies quickly: `Has 2! Mum will make him! But glad ur going. xx.`

Well, this is good. I mean, it would be good if I cared about Drew being there, and if I was going myself. Jess's mum isn't someone you say no to. Jess's mum is Sarah Hartford, who works a lot with the hospital that my mum and Gemma's mum are nurses at. All three of our mums have been work colleagues for years. Sarah Hartford isn't a nurse, though. She runs some care homes for elderly people, ones with big links to the hospital, which is why she deals with Mum a lot – something Mum isn't very happy about. Jess's mum is apparently really fierce about getting the best for her charges. Mum says that no one disagrees with Sarah Hartford. Ever. She has this highly scary way about her.

If Jess's mum makes Drew go to the course, then maybe he really *will* be there. The course isn't school-based – it's off in some forest and you can't get there by bus, so she'll have to drive him, and there aren't exactly any arcades or whatever for him to bunk off to nearby.

'So will you go?' George says, ending his speech.

I think I might give it a go, given this new development. 'Probably not.'

George's face falls. Teasing George is always fun. I reckon this is what having a brother is all about, really.

But he is never down for long. He jumps up and grabs one of his laptops. He has about four, thanks to his dad's

21

job, and he's named them all after his favourite film characters.

'What about if I let you try out Dad's latest game? It's exclusive, you know. I have it here, on Gollum.' He taps the laptop lid gently.

I try not to look too interested. Martin always gets these really cool computer games way before you can buy them – in fact, most of them never seem to make it to the shops at all. They're imports from exotic faraway places, and George's dad is supposed to test them out for the UK market. I think, more often than not, the games totally fail his tests, which is why no one else gets to see them. They're Improvers, like me and Drew, and about as doomed.

Anyway, Martin spends his days trying to break the games so he can report back about how rubbish they are, and sometimes he asks George to help, which means I occasionally get to have a go too.

George smiles at Gollum the Laptop. 'Go on, Lex. It's a good game. It's a bit like those *Sims* games you were addicted to when you were twelve.'

'I wasn't addicted,' I tell him. I remember my cast of cartoon characters who all got busy dating each other and falling out and stuff. Like real life, without the heartache. 'My Sims just had more exciting lives than my real friends, that's all.' This is absolutely untrue, because my real friends were all busy dating each other and falling out and stuff, even then. And even me.

'Well, wait till you see this, then.' George fires up a game and the splash screen reads: *Life, Love, Looks*. It says it's by a company called 'Mystic Inc.', which sounds intriguing too.

'*Life, Love, Looks?* Is that the name of the game?'

George shakes his head. 'No, they're just the three main settings. The game doesn't have an established name yet. Dad says they want to call it *Pygmalions*.'

'Pig-*what*?'

'*Pygmalion* is an ancient story about changing people and making them be what you want them to be. This sculptor fell in love with the statue he created. Dad thinks the title's a bit long to get past Quality Assurance, though. I suggested just *Pygmas* for short.' He taps at the keyboard. 'This is all way too girlie for me, of course. I'm just trying to help Dad.'

I give him a look.

'Oh, all right, I'm thoroughly enjoying it. You can make new avatars – your Pygmas, as I call them, like Sims – from scratch, though. I have two so far—' He clams up. 'Er, oh.'

I'm suspicious. 'Let's see, then.'

George half closes the laptop lid. 'No. Never mind. I forgot I—'

'George. Show me.'

He shakes his head, looking about ten years younger

– around the age he was when he wanted to propose to Jess in the playground with a Hula Hoop.

Now I'm dying to see this game – and find out why George doesn't want me to see it.

'I've changed my mind,' he says.

I think quickly. 'If you let me see, I'll go on the course.'

He looks up. 'Really?'

Well, Mum's going to make me go anyway. Apart from anything else, she doesn't like me hanging around at home alone all day in the school holidays while she's at work. She's probably already arranging for one of her busybody friends to drop in and do random checks on me – or maybe even Martin if she's absolutely desperate. Or else she's finding one of those special activity clubs she always wants me to go to.

Besides, Mr Trench said he would speak to her about it. He's obviously already spoken to Drew's step-aunt, so . . . 'Yeah. Really.'

'OK, then.' George bites his lip. 'Just a sec, though.' He tilts the lid open again and twists the laptop away from me, quickly tapping some keys. Then he lets me see it at last.

The screen is filled with a cartoon image of a girl. She's tall with long, dark, perfectly straight hair. She has a heart-shaped face and a beauty spot on her left cheek. She is absolutely a cartoon version of someone we know

24

well. Besides, the name at the top of the window is a total giveaway.

'You made an avatar to look like Jess?'

'It's a Pygma.'

I snort. Jess is no pig-anything, even in cartoon form.

'Um, yeah, it's supposed to be Jess,' George admits.

I look again. 'It's pretty good, actually. So who's the other one? You said you made two.'

'Promise not to laugh?'

I shrug.

He hesitates for so long that I reach over and click the tile in the corner next to cartoon-Jess. Jess disappears and a cartoon of a boy pops up. He looks film star-ish, a bit like a very young George Clooney, only with more striking eyes. And at the top of the screen it says: GEORGE.

I guffaw.

'Hey! You promised not to laugh!'

'No I didn't. Oh my God, George, is that supposed to be *you*?' I dramatically wipe away invisible tears of laughter. 'It is, isn't it? Ha ha ha!'

'Shut up!' George looks hurt, but he starts laughing too. 'Look, it's supposed to be *based* on me. But actually, everything about it is exactly like me, anyway.' He sniffs. 'I spent ages on it.'

I squint at it, and realize he could be right. Maybe George is quite good-looking, when viewed as a cartoonish avatar. But still . . .

25

'Ha! If it's *exactly* like you, then why has it got such blue eyes? Your eyes are brown!'

George's dark eyes look hunted. 'I might have entered that wrongly.'

He doesn't fool me for a second. 'You mean you might have remembered that conversation Jess had with us in biology last month! When she said she found men with blue eyes attractive!' We were talking about genetics at the time, and George was nearly falling off his chair at the thrill of hearing Jess discussing anything like that. Though if she does, she always says 'men' and not 'boys'.

'Perhaps. Yes,' George admits.

I laugh. 'Oh, *George*.'

'It's only a game!'

Still laughing, I click on the SETTINGS button to the right and look at the list it brings up. The *Looks* menu has lots of sub-lists with things like hair colour, face shape, body shape and distinguishing marks – and also eye colour, which George has set to 'deep blue'. Then I look at the *Life* setting, which has a single slider for 'attitude and outlook', going from 'positive' to 'negative'. George's is set about halfway.

But *Love* is the one that makes me stop laughing and look closer. There are thumbnail images showing the Pygmas, and a drop-down list where you can link them to each other, with tick-boxes labelled KISS, DATE and

26

LOVE. They're the kind of boxes where you can tick more than one, but George hasn't selected any of them. I check Jess's settings and those are blank too. Strange, considering George would probably stop at nothing to get together with Jess, even in a virtual world.

'So do you change the Pygmas' settings if you want them to fall in love? Virtually, I mean?'

'Yes, that's how it's supposed to work. You can choose which Pygmas will 'kiss', 'date' and 'love' each other.' George seems very serious about it. 'I think they're supposed to end up with virtual weddings and everything. Well, if you have the right add-ons. We only have the really basic module and—'

I interrupt him. 'So why haven't you selected yourself in Jess's *Love* settings?'

George avoids my eyes. 'It ... wouldn't be right. Would it?'

'But you changed your eye colour because of what she said.'

'Hmm.' He shifts shiftily.

'George, did you delete your ticks in Jess's *Love* settings just before you showed me this? Did you have Jess set to date you, or kiss you?'

He looks cornered. Then he says, 'Maybe. I might have tried it earlier. But anyway, nothing seems to actually happen in the game, and I've left it for ages. I asked Dad, but he says that's why he'd already decided

27

the game is a no-go. It doesn't work.' He sighs. 'But I can't help thinking that even the Pygma version of me can't get Jess to notice him.'

'Oh, George.' I despair of him. I also understand how he feels. It's like once you feel like that about someone, it's really difficult to switch it off. Like my feelings for Matt. I know I actually went out with Matt, but George has had a thing about Jess for ever and she's barely noticed him. I bet it hurts just as much.

He's looking so sad that I say, 'Look, put it back how it was, if it makes you happy. I don't know why you're bothering to hide it from me, anyway. I *know* you!'

He hangs his head a bit. 'I'm not going to. It really wouldn't be right. Besides, you'll call me pathetic.'

Well, yeah. Of course I will. Though now I'm starting to recognize that I'm just like him. 'Listen, we should make some other girl-Pygmas for Pygma-you to love, to take your mind off Jess.'

'I don't want any other Pygmas – er, girls.'

'George,' I say, 'it's only a game.'

But he's really making me think. I don't want anyone else either! I think I've been sort of trying to talk myself into fancying Drew, almost as a distraction. And OK, Drew is gorgeous, but he's not Matt. Matt is the sporty guy with the easy smile who charms every girl in the school, and even some of the teachers. Matt is effortlessly friendly, and when I was going out with him,

28

everything felt smoother for me too. It's like his laid-back attitude rubbed off on me. Never mind what Gemma said – I should never have broken up with him. She was obviously only trying to put me off him so that she could have him for herself anyway.

Yes, looking at Drew from afar is fun, but it's Matt I want.

If only he wanted me back.

George switches off his laptop, all forlorn, and I catch a glimpse of my reflection in the darkened screen, my expression identical to his.

Oh, we are *both* pathetic!

I stand up. 'Forget them. I mean, *her*. Forget Jess, George. Let's go out.'

I send a quick text to tell Mum I'm studying with Jess and I'll be home late – a white lie I've been telling quite a lot lately, since it means full approval and no questions asked. Then I drag George on the bus to the Bijou, a tiny cinema where we are regulars. It's the kind of place that shouldn't exist any more – in fact, it was derelict until a couple of years ago when this ancient and lovely local film buff called Mike inherited tons of money and poured it all into his dream of owning what he calls 'an independent picture house'. It only has one screen and not really all that many seats, but Mike prides himself on having all the latest technology and loads of subtitled screenings and stuff, and on showing all his favourite

29

culty films. He doesn't seem to care that the place is always practically empty, and spends half his time in the little cinema café (which he calls his 'front room') talking to me and George about how he's 'living the dream' and 'supporting the community through film'.

I know that today the Bijou has a special early showing of one of George's favourite *Lord of the Rings* films, and I think he needs it. At least it replaces his thoughts of Jess with three hours of pure orc-fighting by longhaired men with pointy ears.

I think about Matt the whole time, and how I should never have let Gemma talk me into finishing with him.

As I suspected, Mum gets one phone call from Mr Trench and lays down the law.

'You're going, Lex, and that's final.'

'No way, Mum. I'm not,' I bleat, but my heart's not really in it. I'm starting to think that I *should* go. Maybe, in a different setting, I can start talking to Matt again. Maybe we can sort things out. I can tell him I'm sorry, and that I should never have broken up with him. I could even tell him the truth – that Gemma caused the breakup in the first place, that she was obviously trying to split us up in order to go out with him herself. I'm not sure how he'd take that, though. He might just think I'm trying to stir up trouble between him and Gemma. He might decide that I'm the evil one. But I'd still like the chance to try.

In any case, I go through the motions of a protest campaign with Mum, but then she threatens some special activity week that I *definitely* want to avoid – this one is actually at Mum's hospital and I seriously can't think of anything *worse*. So by the start of the half-term holidays I know I'm definitely going on the film course.

The afternoon before it starts, I'm even a tiny bit excited. I mean, it's film-making, not maths, even if it *is* being taught by Mr Trench. I've always been into films. I'm named after a film character, after all. Mum was watching the dinosaur movie *Jurassic Park* when she went into labour, and she thought it was funny that the child characters had the same surname as us, so she gave me the same first name as the 'clever blonde girl, Lex Murphy'. And she ended up with me: the Improver bald-patch girl, Lex Murphy. It says 'Alexa' on my birth certificate, though, because my nan thought it was a more sensible name and talked Mum into it. But I've always been Lex, except when I'm in trouble.

I'm suddenly weirdly looking forward to this course. I rearrange my hair and practise a little Best Director Oscar acceptance speech in front of the mirror. When I catch myself thanking Trenchie and blubbing, I decide enough is enough and go and join Mum in front of the telly. She doesn't even seem to notice I'm there, she's so engrossed in some reality TV repeat about cosmetic surgery, in which Miss Boobless-And-Proud is confronting Shameless Implant Girl and getting very heated about something I can't make out. I head for the door, shouting to Mum that I'm going to Jess's. But I go to George's instead and Martin answers the door. It's the first time I've seen him out of his office for ages.

'Lex – hello! George says you've been helping out with the bug-testing on one of my games. *Pygmalions*?'

'Yeah, that's right,' I say, though I'd more or less forgotten about the game until now.

'Well, thanks. There are fundamental problems with that one, but George seems determined to keep testing it until it expires at the end of the week. I think he's on it right now. Go on up.'

It's true. George is at his laptop, tapping away intently, when I appear in his doorway.

I say hi, and he jumps a bit and looks up guiltily. 'Wouldn't it be polite to knock?'

'*Hi, Lex, good to see you!*' I prompt him in a silly voice. Then I add, 'Why would I knock? We're practically brother and sister.'

He frowns. 'No we're not. Not at *all*. Anyway, I'm sure sisters ought to knock on their brothers' bedroom doors.'

'I'm sure they, er, ought to not. Or "ought not to", or whatever.' I can't keep up with this Victorian language.

32

'So why are you acting all secretive all of a sudden? Are you perving over cartoon Jess again?'

'Maybe.' He catches himself. 'I mean, no. Not perving. Just, you know . . .'

'Yeah, *I* know. Perving. Budge up.' I shuffle onto the edge of his chair, which is a snug fit for the two of us, even though I'm quite small. George looks uncomfortable.

'Hold on! That's not Jess.' I peer at the screen. It's a skinny girl who looks like an elf with medium-length brown hair. And . . . a clumpy bald patch! Oh my God! 'That's me! Well, me crossed with that girl-elf from *Lord of the Rings*.' I turn to face him.

'You said I should try some other girls.'

'Ugh! George! I didn't mean *me*! That truly *is* pervy! You've made me look like one of your elf crushes.'

'You do look a bit like Arwen Evenstar,' he says nerdishly. 'In real life, I mean. And I do *not* have elf crushes. Though you should say "elven" crushes, and Arwen is actually only half elven.'

'*Whatever!* Oh my God! You haven't attempted to make cartoon-me fall in love with cartoon-you or anything, have you?' This is way too freaky.

'No, of course not,' George says defensively.

'Well, phew.' I nudge him. 'That's all right, then.' He's looking hurt, so I add, 'Hey, as long as you're doing this, why don't we make a few more Pygmas? We could do them for everyone who's supposed to be on the film course. Make them all fall in love with each other and mix things up a bit. Could be a laugh.'

George gives me a knowing look. 'You mean you want to add Drew?'

Oh. No, I was thinking that I wanted to add Matt. But George doesn't know how I feel about Matt. He thinks I'm after Drew, probably because that's what I keep telling him. It's all part of my plan to convince myself, I think. Well, at least it seems to have worked on George. Also, George actually *likes* Drew – he even called him a 'decent fellow' once because Drew held a door open for him, or something like that. In the unlikely event that George and Jess ever actually got together, George liking Drew would be a total problem in their relationship. I've already had to make George swear that he won't tell Jess that I (supposedly) fancy Drew, because I know she'd be furious with me – even if it isn't true.

'I want to add *everyone* from the course,' I say. 'Then they can all have virtual love-ins and adventures on your computer while we're stuck out in the forest.'

George smirks at me. 'I bet you're secretly looking forward to getting lost in the woods with Drew.'

No, I'm secretly looking forward to getting lost in the woods with *Matt*.

'Just shut up and show me how it works, George Clooney Junior.'

So George makes avatars – or Pygmas – for the girls he knows are on the course. He starts with Liana and Teagan, also known as Lia and Tia and, even more commonly, as the Flirt Twins. They're two girls in my year who are kind of like Jess in the brainiac stakes and yet still manage to squeeze in tons of boy craziness in their spare time. They're not actual twins – Liana's dad is Ghanaian and Teagan's family is Irish, for a start – but when Lia joined our school in Year Eight, she and Tia bonded instantly over having rhyming nicknames, and they got even more inseparable when they discovered that they had the same birthday. It's 14 February – yes, Valentine's Day, no joke. Now the Flirt Twins go every-where together, double-dating their way through the hottest boys in school. They've been out with Hayden and Cam too, and also Matt, though it was a long time ago and didn't last long.

'I like Tia's hair,' George says as he selects 'auburn' from the 'hair colour' settings.

I smile. 'There you go, then. Why don't you ask her out?' Though I wonder whether even Tia would say yes. She and Lia are all about image, really, and George is not exactly on their radar.

He looks alarmed. 'I merely said I liked her hair, Lex.' He quickly puts the finishing touches to the Tia avatar, clicks NEW and types *Gemma*.

'Suit yourself,' I mumble, half dreading the creation of

a Pygma Gemma. I hope he doesn't say anything nice about her; I couldn't stand it. I've never talked to George about what happened with her, but sometimes I wonder if he's noticed that we're not very friendly any more. Gemma and I used to be pretty close, and now I barely talk to her, except to make remarks like the one in geography. None of my other friends were in that lesson, but it might have got back to them via the cat-boys. I don't want to think about it.

I bite my lip until George finishes fiddling with Pygma Gemma's blonde mop – he's made her look really pretty, which is accurate, unfortunately. When Gemma and I both decided we fancied our friend Matt, I never thought I'd be the one who actually got together with him.

First, I mean. Ugh.

I relax a bit when George clicks on CREATE and types *Kathryn*.

'Who?' I ask.

He clicks on her profile and pauses. 'She was new this year. Year Ten. I don't know much about her, except that she's on the course.'

News to me. 'How do you even know *that*?'

'I saw it on the sign-up sheet – "Kathryn Ellison" – and she told me who she was yesterday in the lunch queue.' He frowns. 'Then she ran away.' He closes the *Looks* window. 'That's all I know, really. I'll have to fill in the rest when I get more details.'

'More details?' I peer at the screen. 'So, what, you're going to go up to this girl and randomly ask for her date of birth?' I put on a cheesy chat-up voice. *'Heyyy, new girl, what's your siiign?'* I click my fingers. *'I need to know for the settings of my entirely non-pervy cartoon-dating software.'*

George makes a face. 'Forget it. It's not important. I'll leave it blank.'

As soon as he's saved the incomplete Kathryn profile, I announce, 'My turn! Time for some *boys*!'

George moves away and I take the controls. I slowly add Drew, in all his bad-boy hotness. Then I add Hayden and Cam, who are average-looking and fancied by quite a few girls, though Hayden has pretty bad skin and Cam hates his hair colour, aka carrot-top. I give Hayden nice clear skin and lighten Cam's hair so it's closer to blonde. If they knew, I think they'd thank me for that.

Lastly I add Matt, who might not be as gorgeous as Drew on paper (well, on screen), but there's just something about him in real life that makes everyone like him. He's like an advert for sportswear or something – pumped and fit, all upbeat attitude and friendly smiles. I open the *Life* settings and move the 'attitude and out-look' slider to the far left for 'positive'. Matt always looks on the bright side of everything. Even when I dumped him, he only showed signs of being upset for

37

about five seconds. Though he did have Gemma waiting in the wings. Grr.

George, who went to get biscuits when he realized I was going to take ages designing the boys, comes back in and taps me on the shoulder. 'That looks nothing like Matt.'

'Well, how did you know it was him, then?' I retort, even though it does say *Matt* at the top. I still feel indignant about him saying that, though.

'Well, OK, it looks a *bit* like Matt, but . . . enhanced.' George's eyes move from the avatar to me and back a few times, and then he exclaims, 'Oh my goodness, Lex! Please don't tell me you're still in love with Matt?' He knocks the biscuit plate over in alarm.

I catch the biscuits and don't tell him that, or anything else, which doesn't stop him going on.

'But he's— What about Gemma? What about *Drew*?'

I don't say anything. George does enough talking for both of us.

'I know you and Gemma have been strange with each other lately, but I thought it was just the weirdness of her going out with your ex. Anyway, I wasn't worried about it because I didn't think you really cared. Because I thought you were completely over Matt. *You* finished with *him*! And I thought you liked Drew now. You're always talking about him! Have you been lying to me all this time?'

38

'Of course not!' I lie. Well, with a reaction like that, I'm hardly going to tell him the truth, am I? I pick up one of the biscuits and bite into it. The deliciousness of Martin's baking affects my brain because before I can stop myself, I've added, 'He's just so . . . you know.'

George shakes his head like he really doesn't know.

'He's Matt. Everyone thinks Matt is great,' I explain, though surely I don't have to.

George blinks. 'Not everyone.'

Oh. Admittedly, George and Matt have never got on brilliantly, despite being friends, but they're so different that I wouldn't expect them to. I always thought George generally liked Matt, though. Because, as I said, everyone does. And also because . . .

'You never told me you didn't like Matt!'

'That's because you were crazy about him, Lex, and then you went out with him,' George says. 'I'm not completely insensitive, you know. And then, you know . . . well, he's with Gemma now, and she's our friend too.'

I make what I hope is a non-committal sound.

George throws up his arms. 'I'm shocked. I truly can't believe you still carry a torch for Matthew Henderson!'

'I do *what*? What does that even *mean*?'

'It means, Lex, that I don't approve.'

I'm so indignant that I crush part of my biscuit, and George reaches over to brush crumbs frantically off Gollum's keyboard. I frown at his hand. 'Oh? Says the boy who's aiming for virtual marriage to an avatar?'

It's his turn to be affronted. 'I am not! I cleared that setting and I didn't put it back! How could you say that?' Then he gives a dry laugh and stares again at my digitally enhanced Matt avatar. 'Maybe we're as bad as each other.'

'No we're not.' I wolf down the rest of my biscuit in one triumphant crunch. 'Because I am *over* Matt, no matter what you think. If you think I've made the virtual Matt too perfect' – that's because he *is* – 'that's because I haven't finished yet.' I take the controls and mess about with the *Looks* settings until Matt looks more ordinary, and then I open the *Life* settings and move the slider over to 'negative', just for good measure. There. Not so perfect now.

'Better?' I swivel triumphantly in the chair.

George doesn't look convinced.

To avoid facing his lack of conviction, I get busy filling in Matt's 'advanced profile'. It's the screen beyond the main settings, the one that George left blank for Kathryn earlier. You're supposed to enter extra details like date and place of birth, plus additional settings about siblings and pets which are greyed-out and must be intended for the add-ons that George mentioned. I have a go at entering Matt's birthday – a date I remember better than most, seeing as it's the day we first got together using the classic Birthday Kiss technique. (I

40

used it, not him. I seized my chance on his sixteenth. He didn't complain.) I'm typing *23/01* for 23 January, but it keeps being rejected.

'Oh, another bug,' George says, still watching me. 'I'll write it down for Dad, in case he doesn't already have it listed. Though the whole game's pretty much failed anyway.'

'No, hang on.' I remember something, and I try *01/23* instead. 'It's just the wrong way round. It's the American way. Didn't you notice before?'

'I didn't really bother with that bit.' George reaches over and opens his own avatar, navigating to the advanced page, entering his birth date the wrong way round and clicking SAVE AND ACTIVATE. 'Yes, I think you're right. I'll check with the others.'

We fill in advanced profiles for the other Pygmas, though we still have blank boxes for both Drew and Kathryn, the mysterious Year Ten stranger, seeing as they're newbies at our school and they've missed out on the years when everyone learns far too much about everyone else. Pretty soon, we have a complete Pygma set representing every student on Mr Trench's film course.

I contemplate our collection of tiles. 'Now what? Surely it's time to make Jess fall in love with you?'

George sighs. 'It's so tempting.'

'How about if some *other* girls go after Pygma

George?' I suggest. 'Then at least Pygma Jess would notice. She might get jealous and decide you're the Pygma of her dreams.'

George laughs as he shakes his head.

'Never mind,' I say. 'Let's leave the *Love* settings for today.' It's not like I could change Matt's in front of George, even if there was any point in making Matt's avatar fall in love with mine. 'Anyway, your avatar has blue eyes,' I remind him. 'The rest should follow, right?'

George just offers me another biscuit and helps himself to two, staring pensively at his *Lord of the Rings* figurine collection as he munches.

I tinker with my own profile for a bit, wondering about giving myself the long hair I've always wanted, or at least covering up the authentic bald patch George so carefully gave me.

Or I could have a curvier body, so that I can look more like Gemma and less like half an elf. Yes, I like that idea.

I quickly nudge my body-shape settings up a notch when I'm sure George isn't looking, and switch off Gollum the Laptop before he notices.

I think about how great it would be if you could change yourself so easily in real life. And other people too.

The next morning, the first day of the film course, I'm late reaching George's house. It takes me ages to get dressed, and not just because I want to choose the perfect Matt-attracting outfit. Mostly it's because nothing seems to fit me properly. Everything feels uncomfortable and tight, especially my bra! I must ask Mum for money for a new one. I must also lay off Martin's delicious biscuits, just in case they've made me swell up overnight. Or maybe I'm finally growing Gemma-like curves, though I don't know why my body had to pick today for a sudden growth spurt. I decide to go bra-less, even though this feels a bit weirder than it used to. Why did nobody warn me there could be a downside to developing the figure I've always wanted?

At least I managed to get Mum to agree that Martin could drive me to the course. When I asked her the other day, she tutted a bit and muttered about 'that man'. Then she said she supposed she had no choice because *she* had to work, unlike *some* people who sat about in their houses all day. This is just one of the things that Martin and Mum obviously argued about in their short relationship. Mum is incredibly sensitive about the fact that she's a single parent in a semi she wouldn't be able to afford if it wasn't for all the help Nan gave her back when she got pregnant in her late teens. Another problem she has with Martin is that he's clearly never needed any help from his parents – in fact he has no parents any more – and yet his side of the house is all done up and double glazed, whereas our half is visibly

43

falling apart because Nan doesn't have any money left now either.

We're almost at the forest, with Martin's posh dad-car smoothly negotiating the steep hill that always makes Mum's car shudder and shake, when I notice that George is looking at me oddly. Up until now we've been sitting in friendly silence, the kind that comes easily between me and George, what with the whole practically-brother-and-sister thing. I expect he's been thinking about Jess, though. And I know I've been thinking about Matt. We're still the same sad cases we were last night on the computer.

Meanwhile, even though I can't make out a word of it from the back seat, I know Martin has been keeping up a monologue about gaming software. I know it because that's what he always does. Sometimes I wonder what he and Mum ever talked about, though I swear she was happy with him before it all went wrong.

But now I notice that George is staring at me. His gaze is aimed at my chest, which is very weird.

I wave my hand in his eye-line. 'Hello? I'm up here!'

He goes bright red. 'Oh God! Sorry! I didn't mean to . . . There's, um, something different about you.'

He's picked a fine time to turn into a sleaze! I glare at him. And then I frown. 'There's definitely something different about *you*.'

George glances down at himself. He's wearing a

44

tweedy jacket, shirt and trouser combo that wouldn't look out of place on Mr Trench himself. He looks slightly messier than usual, though, like he got dressed in a rush and didn't look in the mirror.

'No, not your crap clothes,' I tell him. He knows what I think of his fashion sense and it doesn't bother him – he insists it's the only style that suits him. I suggest he'd be better off wearing school uniform.

I realize what's different. 'I mean your eyes.'

He rubs at them. 'I couldn't get to sleep last night. Nerves. Then I overslept this morning.'

'I don't mean the enormous messenger bags under them, George. I mean their colour.' I glance around. We're turning into the large car park at the edge of the forest, and the trees are pretty thick already. 'It must be the weird light in here.'

'What are you talking about, Lex?'

'I mean your eyes look . . . blue.' I squirm in my too-tight clothes and wonder about having developed extra curves overnight. 'Deep blue.'

George gets it before I do, and he frowns. 'You mean, like the setting in the game?'

I don't answer, because it's crazy – and impossible.

But . . . yes. Blue like the setting in the game. Curvy like my body shape in the game.

I think about George telling me the game is a failure because the changes don't work.

'Nah, it's just the light,' I tell him.

The alternative is far too bizarre.

We get out of the car and head for the meeting place. I'm fizzing inside, feeling secretly glad I'm on this course after all. Never mind Matt, or Drew, or boys in general – this is something I'm really interested in. I've done the right thing, agreeing to this.

How *stupid* was I, agreeing to this?

Not only do I have to suffer George making soppy eyes at Jess and turning red if she glances in his direction for a second and looks right through him. But it's slowly sinking in that – OMIGOD WHAT WAS I THINKING, AM I INSANE? – I am also stuck with Evil Gemma Grant and the annoying Mr Trench ALL WEEK.

'Welcome to Base Camp. HAR HAR!' Mr Trench says in his booming Teacher Voice.

Jess actually laughs at Trenchie's total non-joke.

Insanity, meet Lex Murphy. My movie namesake used her wits to help people escape from a dinosaur island. Who will help me escape from here?

Matt is in the room with me, of course. But he has Evil Gemma right next to him, emanating demon rays that form a protective barrier around her precious boyfriend. We're sitting in a circle and Gemma keeps stroking Matt's arm and inching her chair closer to his. I think I detect him pulling away from her a bit but I must be imagining it, because he'd never do that. He and Gemma are sickeningly in love, and they're even more under my nose than usual. Why did I ever think this week could change anything? It's hopeless.

Ms Cosgrove is also here, assisting Mr Trench. It turns out she was on a training course with him: 'Teaching Digital Media and Ruining Half Term', or whatever its official title was. Things could not possibly get much worse than this.

'It's great to see you all here and MOTIVATED,' Old Trenchie booms. 'It's going to be an intensive week. There's a tremendous amount of WORK that goes into even the shortest piece.'

'And fun too,' Ms Cosgrove adds.

Mr Trench glares at her with his steely blue eyes. 'Hard WORK,' he says. 'Graft. Be prepared for one of the toughest weeks of your LIVES. And the most rewarding.' At this point he stares mostly at me. Huh! He always thinks I need more 'rewarding'. I always think I need more 'being left completely alone'.

As soon as he starts talking again, I roll my eyes at Jess but I don't know why I bother. She's staring at Mr Trench, sitting up as straight as her perfect, gleaming dark hair. It looks even shinier than usual today. How does she manage it? I know for a fact she doesn't put the time in with the ultra-expensive shampoo and the boring straighteners. She just gets up in the morning looking like that, and she doesn't even care – she's entirely focused on her love of schoolwork. Life's so unfair. Then I think about my sudden curves, and George's blue eyes, and I wonder whether I could try giving myself instant Jess-hair too.

And I wonder whether I could make Matt want to go out with me again.

Then I wonder whether I'm actually insane for wondering these things.

I glance at Hayden, whose skin looks clearer today. And Cam, who's definitely looking blonder. But it must be acne cream, hair dye and/or a trick of the light.

I try rolling my eyes at George instead of Jess, but he's too busy doing a lovesick-puppy impression at her to notice me. Oh, brother.

'Alexa Murphy, I'm terribly sorry to keep you from the more pressing matters of COMMUNICATING with your posse,' Trenchie booms at me.

Gemma sniggers evilly.

Yeah. Ha *very* ha. I reckon they have a normal-humour removal session on day one of teacher-training college. It gets replaced with Teacher Humour, and they get tested on it and everything. Trenchie probably got an A-star in that exam.

Anyway, I'm sure Mr Trench feels right at home here. It's pretty obvious that Base Camp (Har Har), which is basically a hut at the edge of the forest, used to be some kind of teen prison. The sign on the door says CENTRE FOR BEHAVIOURALLY CHALLENGED YOUNG PEOPLE – a bit like Trenchie's 'Improvers' – and the walls are papered with interesting slogans like, *Respect yourself!*, *Think it, don't say it!* and *Count to ten before you act!*

But there's only one behaviourally challenged young person/Improver here: me. Drew has not turned up, and even though it's typical of him, I'm crushingly disappointed. Wasn't Jess's mum supposed to force him to attend? I tried asking Jess about him when we first got here – but casually, so that she wouldn't think I fancied Drew, which I don't, of course. She just sighed and said, 'Oh, my annoying step-cousin! He is a major *pain*! Oh, Lex, I'm so excited about this course!' and then she babbled on for half an hour about what she hoped she'd learn from Mr Trench. So I have no idea how Drew got past Jess's mum, leaving me cooped up in a Young Offenders' prison with Evil Gemma, Trench Mouth, barmy old Cosmic Cosgrove, ultra-boffin Jess and lovestruck George. Oh, and Matt, with Gemma sticking to him like a limpet.

At least we're sitting in this diplomatic, un-school-like circle, and Ms Cosgrove and Mr Trench are in off-duty mode. Mr Trench is actually wearing shorts. (Ugh, don't look – teacher legs!) Ms Cosgrove is wearing rainbow-coloured floaty clothes, as usual, because teaching geography makes her automatically wafty and at one with nature, communing with clouds.

Mr Trench does a big throat-clearing thing, complete with under-chin slapping. Great – what wisdom is he about to impart now?

But Ms Cosgrove speaks instead. She must have booked Mr Trench as her phlegmy attention-getter. 'I want you to think of yourselves as a team! A production team!' She beams at us and then at Mr Trench, challenging him to join in with her.

He stretches his face into a grimace, like a politician on daytime telly. It must be tough for him, poor man, trying to be nice to us for a change.

Ms Cosgrove opens her arms wide, as if she's about to hug us all. I squirm into my chair.

'Yes, that's you! The production team! This is going to be so much fun. We're embarking on an exciting project! The sky's the limit! And we're *together* on this adventure.'

Jess smiles excitedly at Mr Trench. George smiles excitedly at Jess.

I remember a film I once saw where, at the end, this man escaped a mental hospital by smashing the window and making a run for it.

I locate the windows and scan the room for blunt instruments. There's a huge pile of cameras in a box behind Ms Cosgrove.

'OK, first things first. This is an intensive course—'

'So daily attendance is VITAL,' Mr Trench interrupts.

'Yes,' Ms Cosgrove agrees, 'but I don't think that will be a problem once you see what we have in store for you over the next five days. We'll be focusing on various aspects of film-making, starting with . . .' She goes on. And on. And also, just for good measure, on.

My nails are fascinating. Why does the polish chip right off some of them and stay on others? There's a pink half-moon left on my thumbnail. What does it all *mean*? I wonder if there have been scientific studies in this stuff. I wonder if you need a university degree to work in the nail-varnish industry. Probably. Jess would know. Jess isn't looking at her nails – she's still firmly fixed on Ms Cosgrove. Why can't I be more like Jess? It must be great to be able to concentrate on stuff.

I rest my head on my hands and try to keep my eyes open and focused on the moving Cosgrovian mouth.

'And we'll end with a screening of a piece of group work, which will amount to a short trailer-style summary of the course – an advert to attract future students and a taster for the weekly club we'll start at school after the holidays.' This gets my attention, though not as much as the next thing Ms Cosgrove says: 'The final screening will be very special. All your families are invited, and so are the local press. Thanks to the kind permission of the owner, it'll be held at the Bijou cinema in town.'

I exchange a glance with George, and he mouths at me, *Our cinema!*

Wow! It will probably be the biggest crowd Mike has attracted since he held his retro Austin Powers night, and George and I were joined in the audience by a couple of psychedelic dad-types who thought they were cool.

Everyone else stirs at the news too, and Jess starts to panic. 'But how can we make anything good enough to show the *press*? In less than a week!' Her eyes grow wide. 'We don't know anything about film-making!'

'*Yet*. You'll be surprised,' Ms Cosgrove soothes. 'Besides, it's a showcase – it doesn't have to be perfect.'

Jess looks like she's having a heart attack. She doesn't do Not-Perfect.

'But first things first. Today we need to familiarize ourselves with the equipment.'

Mr Trench bends down towards a large pile of electrical stuff. He hands the Cosmic One a stick with a fluffy pouch-type thing on the end.

'Who can suggest a use for this?' The Cosmic One waves the stick about.

Mr Trench chooses that moment to bend down and move a box.

I decide to *think it and not say it*.

'It's a microphone with a boom,' says my perfect-student friend.

'Very good, Jess,' crows Ms Cosgrove. 'And this?' She holds up what can only be described as, um, a camera.

'A camera,' Gemma says.

Give the girl a GCSE.

'That's right, Gemma,' says Ms Cosgrove.

Gemma always used to say she couldn't see the point of learning anything that didn't lead to a 'proper career' like our mums'. Maybe she's changed her mind about nursing now that she's realized that pure Evil like hers has no place in a caring profession.

She turns to Matt and beams with pride. Evil, evil. Evil Gemma Grant. Initials: EGG. Eggy Evil Gemma Grant.

'Nice one, Gem,' Matt says, though he looks a bit bored and sarcastic, for him. Weird. I must be imagining it.

Cosmic Cosgrove goes on and on, slowly introducing every snore-some piece of equipment, complete with a special focus on 'the battery compartment' and – ooh, excitement, fanfare – 'the *battery*' itself, before she does a lengthy demonstration of How To Switch The Camera On. It's going to be a long week.

I scan the room again. I can't look at Gemma and Matt. Which absolutely doesn't explain why I *am* looking. I force my eyes away. Jess is perky and shiny-eyed on the edge of her seat. George is scribbling something in a notebook – probably his latest Jess-luring strategy combined with a detailed map of Middle Earth. Lia and Tia are nudging each other and whispering. Hayden and Cam are doing the boy equivalent of that, i.e. shoving each other and swearing under their breath. The Year Ten girl we don't know very well, Kathryn, is staring into space. I'm close to falling off my chair in extreme slouchdom and DREW IS NOT HERE. Why not? He would at least bring a hint of originality to the room.

'So what I need you to do, as an initial familiarization task, is to get into pairs and venture out into the woods.' Our teacher nods at each of us in turn. 'Explore your equipment and environment as much as possible.' Uh-huh, figures. 'Environment' is definitely Ms Cosgrove's favourite word, though we like to joke that it's 'cosmos' or 'cosmic', as they go better with her name. That's probably the reason she became a geography teacher – limitless opportunities to use words like that. 'So I'll assign you each a partner and distribute the equipment,' she finishes.

'I'm with Matt!' Gemma squeaks.

Yes, yes, Egg-face, we all know that.

'OK, Gemma's with Matt,' Cosmic Cosgrove says.

Sometimes I think there's some kind of conspiracy, with the whole world rubbing my face in the fact that those two are together.

'Whatever,' Matt seems to say, but I must be

misunderstanding him, as he looks so . . . not bothered.

'Kathryn darling, you pair with Jess. George, you go with . . .' Cosmic nods at me vaguely. Strange – she didn't have a problem remembering my name when I was 'disrupting' her lesson. Maybe my new curves have made me look totally different. Or maybe she doesn't recognize me when I'm not turning boys into miaowing cats.

'ALEXA MURPHY,' Mr Trench booms from the back of the room. It's so familiar that it almost makes me feel cosy.

George gives me a little smile, but I know he's disappointed that he's paired with me.

'Liana and Teagan can work together,' Ms Cosgrove continues. 'Is that OK?'

The Flirt Twins smile. Of course it is.

'Hayden and Cam – you're partners.'

They certainly are. So far, so every day at school. I wish there was someone here who could shake things up a bit.

Drew, Drew, where are yew?

'And the latecomer . . .' Cosmic glances at a sheet of paper, 'Andrew Ashton might have to join one of the other pairs, but Mr Trench can be his partner for now.'

Oh, poor Drew. If he hears about that, he definitely won't turn up tomorrow, either.

'I meant to ask earlier – does anyone here know the

WHEREABOUTS of Andrew Ashton?' Mr Trench booms.

I couldn't have boomed it better myself.

'Drew overslept this morning,' Jess pipes up in her prim, talking-to-teachers way. 'Mum said we'd be late if we waited for him, so she's driving him here in a bit.'

Ah! Mystery solved. Oversleeping? Drew is a genius. Sometimes the simple escape routes are the best. Though he probably didn't do it on purpose. Knowing him, he was probably at some wild party all night.

'OK. So does everyone know who they're working with?' Ms Cosgrove checks.

'Ahem, actually, would it be possible for me to work with . . . Jess?' George says, not half as hesitantly as he should, considering he's brutally and publicly ditching his almost-sister. How can he do this to me? Not to mention the fact that he's just clearly announced his love for Jess, who totally hasn't noticed, as usual. To Jess, George is wallpaper.

'I think that *could* be possible . . .' If Ms Cosgrove's expression was a shampoo, it would be called something like Soft 'n' Generous. 'But *why*, George?'

'Because I . . . uh . . .' He can't think of anything. 'Lex doesn't . . . She should . . .'

I glare at him. He can leave *me* out of it!

He gives up, his expression awash with the shampoo of shame. 'Sorry.'

His eyes still look blue. My clothes still feel tight. If you really *can* change people through the settings of a game, then I might turn him into a monster later. Or an orc.

'Well, let's see. Does anyone else want to change partners?' Ms Cosgrove asks, displaying an understanding that George has given her absolutely no good reason to deserve.

'I'm with Matty,' Gemma simpers, linking her puny arm through Matt's burly one.

Urrrgh.

My only consolation is that Matt doesn't seem to be smiling. At all. In fact, his expression is positively moody, which is an odd look for him, especially when he's around *her*.

Mr Trench strides closer. 'ERRRR, let's all stick to the ORIGINAL pairings that Ms COSGROVE decided!' he booms. He adds, 'Or else she'll get confused.'

Cosmic goes bright red and fiddles with a sequin that's hanging by a thread from her skirt. 'OK, right, folks. Cameras!'

'Action,' says Kathryn. It's the first thing she's said all morning, apart from whispering her name when we 'introduced ourselves' to each other at the start, which was a bit of a joke seeing as we've mostly all known, dated, hated, ignored and/or lusted after each other for years. Except Kathryn, of course, who's as new as Drew.

We all stare at her.

She shrinks back into her chair.

Ms Cosgrove smiles at her kindly as she hands out cameras in bags. 'Kathryn and Jess, here's yours. Gemma and Matt. George and Alexa.'

'Lex,' I correct.

'Alexa,' Mr Trench confirms, because a shortened name is a sure route to hooliganism. I wish for escape. I look at the door.

And, like magic, it opens, and a tall, scruffy, lush boy slopes in.

Drew! I made him appear through the power of my thought. Amazing. Shows anything can happen if you want it desperately enough. So maybe I *can* get back with Matt.

Oh, help, I am seriously confused.

'Sorry I'm late and stuff.' Drew shrugs. Even with that one laid-back sentence his mouth movements are super sexy, and I de-slouch on my chair by at least two slump-notches.

'Ah, Mr Ashton, I presume?' Mr Trench says, quoting 'Joke' 29 in the Manual of Teacher 'Humour', which has to be standard issue from teacher-training college. 'Nice of you to join us.' That'll be 'Joke' 2.

Ms Cosgrove smiles at Drew. 'Welcome to the workshop. It's going to be an exciting week . . .' She launches into the same dull speech she gave the rest of us a few minutes ago.

Drew walks over to Jess, completely ignoring Ms Cosgrove.

'Young MAN!'

And completely ignoring the booming Mr Trench.

Well, *this* was worth waiting for. I sit up even straighter.

'Yo, cuz.' Drew flicks Jess on the shoulder.

Jess winces prettily.

'Master Ashton, please be SEATED!'

There is one spare chair in our Base Camp Har Har circle, but it's between Kathryn and Matt, and near the teachers.

'Over HERE,' Mr Trench points out indignantly.

'Sure,' Drew says, 'but I need to check with my seating consultant first.' His eyes flash comically at me as he asks, 'Lex, are the chairs safe in this place?'

Drew is magnificent. The scruffy hair, the lanky limbs. That grin. The way he's totally disrespecting Mr Trench. The way he's smiling at me. 'Maybe I need to share a seat,' he says, 'just to be on the safe side.'

Does he mean *with me*? I glance at Matt, wondering what he thinks of this. Does he ever think about me at all any more? But Gemma's whispering something to him, something evil, and he's staring at the ground.

'ANDREW ASHTON!'

'It's Drew.' He meets our fearsome leader's eyes, totally fear-free.

59

Trenchie is spitting words now. 'Andrew, I realize you are relatively new and UNFAMILIAR with the DISCIPLINE expected by me, even off the official school premises, but nevertheless I must STRESS . . .'

Drew perches casually on the edge of Jess's seat and she shifts away from him. He leans forward, putting his head in his hands as if he's fascinated by what Mr Trench is saying.

'It may be the half-term HOLIDAYS, but—'

'Aha. No problem, Teach. It's cool.' Drew shrugs again. 'I'll behave myself.'

If Mr Trench clutched his heart and staggered around right now, I wouldn't be surprised.

Cosmic flaps her notepad. 'Er, Andrew, I think you should have a seat to yourself.'

'That's all right, thanks. I'm comfortable here.' Drew stretches his long legs out in front of him and grins at me again.

Jess smiles tightly, as if to apologize for her terrible cousin. She wears that expression a lot when Drew's around. 'It's OK, Ms Cosgrove, I'll move,' she says, getting up and walking over to the empty seat. 'Kathryn's my partner, after all.'

Kathryn glances shyly at her through a long curtain of fringe.

Ms Cosgrove looks uncertain. 'I suppose it makes sense.'

'Hey, Lex,' Drew says, settling into Jess's former chair and leaning over in a friendly sort of way. 'You got a partner?'

He is gorgeous. I really think I might be in love with Drew as well as Matt.

In the split-second that follows, nearly everyone stares at me, including George with his freaky blue eyes.

But not including Matt. Though Matt seems to have detached himself completely from Gemma now. Is the perfect couple in trouble? Is this my chance?

Meanwhile Drew is waiting for an answer to his thrillingly double-meaning-ish question (if you read too much into it – which I feel like doing, the way he's looking right now).

I am utterly confused.

If I say anything remotely flirty to Drew, though, I think Jess might possibly stop talking to me for ever out of sheer horror. I'm not sure whether I care – at least, not right now.

On the other hand, I know Drew probably doesn't mean anything by it. It's the kind of thing that lads like him do all the time: effortless, meaningless flirting. I've lost one friend over a boy recently – even though it's entirely Gemma's fault that I don't speak to her – and I'm not risking losing Jess too. I pull myself together.

I glance at Matt again – there's something *strange* about him today – before I say firmly to Drew, 'I'm with

61

George.' I feel an odd need to repeat myself. 'George is my partner.'

Drew shrugs and his eyes lose their sparkle, and now I think I imagined the flirtiness. I'm not sure whether I feel let down about that or not.

'Master Ashton will need to accompany ME, in any case,' Trenchie booms. 'He has missed our introduction and therefore he has no idea how his EQUIPMENT works.'

Drew actually seems to cringe a bit in the nudging and giggling that follows, which is cute.

'As for the rest of you, I'd like you to FAMILIARIZE yourselves with the handheld cameras, using the specific settings I showed you EARLIER.'

Uh-oh. Earlier? I hope George was listening.

Ms Cosgrove takes over. 'As you explore the settings, I want to set you a special mission too. Try to film the changing light. Find the tones of the forest. Find the darkness as well, and capture it.'

It all sounds like one of George's favourite films.

Mr Trench can't resist barking another order over the Cosmic woolliness. 'Stay in your PAIRS, and we'd like you back here in FORTY minutes to screen your findings.'

'Don't be afraid to experiment with sound and pictures,' Ms Cosgrove warbles, making gentle waves with her arms. 'Examine the flora and fauna of the forest and—'

Mr Trench cuts her off. 'Ms Cosgrove, I need you to pay a visit to the suppliers in town for a small amount of stock.' I can't believe he orders *her* about too. Teachers are power-crazed. 'Off you GO, students!'

Drew turns to me through the scuffle of chairs. 'What did I do to deserve this?'

I half smile at him, but I'm watching Matt and Gemma. They seem to be having some kind of hissy, silent row on their way out of the room. There's definitely some trouble brewing there.

Interesting.

The other team-mates pair off and mill about, fiddling with their cameras. Lia and Tia clearly think they're in training for an Olympic giggling event. Hayden and Cam are holding some kind of burping contest. Jess and Kathryn are at the door and have probably shot half their film and got an Oscar nomination already. Drew slopes over to Mr Trench, and George bounds up to me.

'Hurry, Lex,' he says. 'We need to follow them!' He cuddles the camera that Ms Cosgrove issued. 'This is the week me and Jess get together. It's going to happen! I'll do whatever it takes. I am *determined*!' He underlines this with serious eyes, and I do another double-take at their colour.

I wonder about the game again – is that why George's eyes are blue and my bra is tight?

I watch Matt disappear into the forest with Gemma

and wonder about the *Love* settings on George's game: *Kiss*, *Date*, *Love*. Could I use the game to get things back to how they were between me and Matt, only . . . better?

No, I couldn't. For that is absurd.

But I really want to try.

About half an hour later, I think it's safe to announce that George and I are not going to get a BAFTA for our first assignment.

'Are you sure this is what we're supposed to be doing?' I ask him. I mean, I didn't catch everything the teachers said earlier, but I'm pretty sure that hiding behind a tree and spying on girls wasn't mentioned even once. 'Shouldn't we be filming stuff?'

'I *am* filming!' says George, keeping the camera focused on the clearing where, in the distance, Jess is pointing her camera at the ground. She's probably making a BBC4 feature-length documentary about the emotional life of an ant, or something. She looks really serious and intense about what she's doing.

To be fair, so does George. It's just that I don't think filming Jess standing prettily by a tree while Kathryn takes control of the camera is exactly what Ms Cosgrove had in mind.

'George, you can't just keep filming *Jess*.'

'I'm not! I'm filming the . . . tree?' He thinks about it. 'Yes, I'm filming the tree.'

'The tree that has Jess leaning against it.'

'Lucky tree.' George gives a defeated sigh and puts the camera down, resting it on his leg. He pouts like a little boy. 'But this is what we were told to do! I'm merely experimenting with the camera. Examining the, er, cosmos.'

I nod. 'OK, so are you going to tell Cosmic Cosgrove that the natural fauna of the forest includes sixteen-year-old girls? And what about when Mr Trench makes us show our footage to the whole group when we get back?' I punctuate that with another, more knowing nod. 'Because he will, you know.'

George goes white. 'You're right, Lex.' Then he wails, 'Why didn't you stop me?'

I look at my non-existent wrist-watch. 'I've been trying to for the past half-hour.'

He checks his real-life wrist-watch. 'But there isn't much time now! What are we going to do? I need to impress her!'

I sigh. 'Give it here.' I take the camera and get some shots of the sky through the trees. I've been watching George for long enough to know what to do and which buttons to press, but in any case it feels weirdly natural to have a camera in my hand. I've always wanted to try stuff like this, but I could never ask Mum for anything as expensive as a proper camera. She's not made of money, which doesn't grow on trees, etc. Besides, I'm enough of a problem for her without adding me-related money worries to the list. She wouldn't say that last part, ever, of course. But I know she thinks it.

After a couple of minutes I speed-play back the footage, including George's. Ninety-nine per cent of it is back-to-back Jess: Jess walking, Jess laughing, Jess looking at the sky. Jess, Jess, Jess.

'I'm deleting *all* this,' I tell him. 'Unless you want Jess to see it.'

George looks doubtful. Then he looks hopeful. 'But maybe it would be OK if she did. I mean, it would send her a clear sign, wouldn't it?'

'Yes,' I agree, but I wipe the hope off his face by adding, 'A sign of complete desperation.'

Though if I could send Matt coded signs about how I feel through the medium of film, then I totally would. I'd start with: *Sorry – I wish I hadn't broken up with you.*

'Sorry,' I say to George instead – his face has fallen so far it's practically on the ground. 'But it's not the best sign.'

He sighs. 'So what *is*? I've tried everything.'

'That's just it, George. You should probably stop trying. Show Jess you don't care. Flirt with some other girls. Get them interested in you. Show her what she's missing – make her jealous.' Is this what I've been doing with Drew? Matt moved on so quickly. I want it to look like I did too. Right before we get back together.

66

'Flirt? *Me*?' George's mouth is etched with misery. 'Lex, *how*? With *whom*?'

I roll my eyes because guys who say 'whom' do not get the girl of their dreams and he will never learn. 'Just girls, you know. Any of them. *All* of them. Show Jess how popular you are.'

'But I'm not!'

By George! 'OK, forget it. Let's just find something great to film.' I can at least show Matt what I can do.

'You mean something to impress her?'

'Yes, and him,' I say without thinking.

George considers me with his blue eyes. 'You mean Matt, don't you?'

'Um, no,' I mumble. Stupid computer game, making George suspect the truth.

'Well, you obviously don't mean Drew, judging by how you spoke to him back at the hut.'

This startles me. 'That doesn't mean I don't like him! I do! Drew's gorgeous.' I am instantly all confused again.

George's expression probably matches mine. We are the Confusion Twins.

'Look, I only meant I don't want to get into trouble with Trenchie.' And then, before he can call me on my obvious lie – I mean, since when have I worried about *that*? – I switch the camera to RECORD and start carefully filming some tree bark, moving away from George. I switch the fancy effects on so that I get tree bark in black and white, tree bark in negative that looks like tree bark from outer space, and tree bark that mirrors back on itself and makes me feel a bit sick. We can call this biopic *The Chronicles of Tree Bark*, a forgotten chapter of *The Lord of the Rings*.

George is totally missing my Tolkien-inspired genius. He's gazing off towards Jess again with a stupid expression on his face. I walk back, ducking under some trees and filming him as I approach, capturing those deep blue eyes.

Then something makes me stop. I grab George's arm and say in what I hope is a really quiet voice, 'I sensed something . . . Weird movement in the trees.'

He mouths back, *What?*

'Can't you hear anything?'

'No. You're scaring me! What is it? A beast? A werewolf? A monster?' He pauses. 'Hold on – I think I heard it. It's just a girl giggling.' He squints at a nearby tree. 'Gemma, I think.'

'Gemma and Matt?' No wonder it made me shudder.

'I only heard Gemma.'

I peer. I can see the outline of a fluffy pink coat now. Gemma's coat – I was with her when she bought that, on one of our Saturdays when we were still proper friends. She's under the tree and she's with someone. I really don't want to see her and Matt together like this. But for some stupid reason I point the camera at her and press the zoom.

The first thing I notice is that the person she's with is wearing a black leather jacket.

And I'm pretty sure Matt wasn't wearing anything like that earlier. He doesn't even own anything leather, as far as I know. He's a football-kit boy all the way, when he's not in coolly scruffy stuff for school.

I shift a bit but I still can't see their faces. George is looking at me strangely. I whisper, 'Who do you think she's with?'

He goes pompous. 'Er, Lex, weren't you telling me off for spying about five minutes ago?'

'Ssh! Who?'

He hesitates. 'I thought I heard a male voice. Scottish accent.'

'Drew?' Omigod, it's Drew.

George nods.

Gemma's with Drew.

Why is *Gemma* with *Drew*? She and Matt are joined at the hip! What is going on? Did they fall out? And what could she be saying to Drew? Is she warning him off me because she thinks I've 'gone psycho lately', as she said during that incident in geography?

Or is she *after* him – the way she must have been after Matt the whole time I was going out with him? Is she determined to go for any boy I ever like?

I struggle to control my voice. 'Why would Gemma be with Drew? Matt's her partner. Drew was with Mr Trench.'

George shrugs. 'Maybe they swapped for some reason.'

'Like what? Can you make out anything they're saying?'

'Lex, don't worry about it.'

But I *am* worrying. It's no good being confused about whether I like Drew or Matt if Gemma's gone off with *both* of them anyway. How does she *do* this? Was she only put on this planet to ruin my life?

Plus now I think I might hate Drew after all. He made me think he liked me, even if he was just playing. But he knows I got into trouble for fighting with Gemma. What is he *doing* with her?

George touches my shoulder. 'You OK, Lex?'

'Yeah, no. Like I care, anyway. Let's go.' I walk away and George follows me.

'May I see what you filmed?' he asks me in his Victorian-gentleman way.

I hand him the camera and he replays *The Chronicles of Tree Bark*. He's quiet for ages. Then he says, 'That's fabulous, Lex.'

I shrug. 'I was just experimenting.'

He nods. 'Well, I don't think we need to worry about it being shown to the group. I think we'll impress them

with this.' He goes a bit shifty. 'So anyway . . . I wanted
to say . . . I should tell you . . .'

'What?'

He seems to reconsider, or maybe this pathetic statement is what he was working up to: 'I can't see where
Jess is any more.'

My skin prickles with irritation. I feel so disappointed
in Drew, and Gemma, and Matt, and everyone.

And George will not stop going on about Jess!

'She must have gone that way.' He points into the
distance. 'Can we look for her?'

Every nice bone in my body floods with meanness
that overflows into my words. 'George, this is hopeless.
Don't you get it? It's *never* going to happen between you
and Jess!'

The same way Matt will never want me back and
Drew isn't interested in me after all. The only person
who gets what she wants every time is Gemma. The
whole world revolves around *Gemma*.

George looks horrified now, but it's too late. I can't
take it back. And anyway, I'm really talking to myself,
not him. I should give up on Matt, and Drew, and boys
in general, if Gemma's around. 'Oh, forget it. I'm sorry,
but this course is a waste of time. I'm going home.'

I stomp towards Base Camp Har Har. I don't care
what Mum says – I'm going to spend my week watching daytime telly and stuffing my face with crisps, like I

71

originally planned. Starting now. I can't get out of here fast enough. I almost break into a run, but it's difficult because the path is uneven and I'm crushing crunchy bits of wood underfoot and stumbling over pine cones.

The ground shakes behind me and I turn. George is gaining on me. He catches up and grabs my arm. 'Lex, calm down! How will you get home? There are no buses and your mum's out all day!'

'I'll think of something. I'll hitch a lift!'

'Promise me you won't! It's dangerous! Listen, at least call my dad, or I'll come with—'

'Are you saying I can't look after myself?' Anger makes my head pulse. 'I don't need you, George!'

I turn, and this time there's a short thud followed by nothing. He's not following me. That's it – I've done it now. I've chased away my final friend. And I *do* need George. Why did I say that?

I take a few more steps, but an uncomfortable feeling makes me stop and turn round, and then I see why George isn't following me. He's in a heap on the ground by a giant rotten log. He seems to be howling at an invisible moon. 'Owwww! Ow-ow-owwwwww!'

I shrug away my bad mood and walk over. I should probably apologize, but George is still holding the camera, and somehow a joke comes out instead. 'Is this part of the project? Are you filming yourself pretending to be a wolf? To wow Jess?'

'At least I saved the camera!' George wails. 'Lex, thank God you're back. I need you!'

'Well, yeah . . .' I give him a soppy grin. 'I wouldn't be without you either. I'm sorry about what I said before. I didn't mean it.' I lean down and attempt a bear hug.

He winces. 'Thanks, I know you didn't. But what I mean is, I *need* you. Because I tripped over that branch and I think I've broken my leg!'

George's accident changes the whole of the film course.

At first I don't think he can really have any broken bones because, at my suggestion, he gets up and makes a pretty good job of leaning on me and hobbling back towards Base Camp Har Har. If anything was fractured, wouldn't he be passing out and unable to move at all?

It takes ages, though, and after a while I start to worry. I'm no expert on medical matters even though I've hung around hospitals a lot in my lifetime – not only because that's where Mum works but also from being an in-patient with meningitis, and all my various check-ups and appointments afterwards. I decide to try a quick bit of nurse-style analysis on George. He does look pretty grey, and he's insisting he can't put any weight on his left foot at all. Instead, he's leaning heavily against my new, curvier body, which feels highly weird.

I wonder whether I should have let him even try to move. It's probably made everything worse, and he'll have to have his leg cut off now or something. And it will be my fault if George loses a limb, and Martin might get properly angry for a change instead of sadly resigned and slightly guilty, like he is over the thing that split up him and Mum. Mum might even side with him over this one. Then I'll be cast out of my home and have to find a new family who don't look out for each other and eat each other for breakfast. Like Gemma's, for example. She's now on her third hideous step-dad in a row, and I'd feel sorry for her if she wasn't so evil.

George winces again, confirming my fate. 'Can we have a rest?'

We stumble to a nearby tree stump and he sits down, extending his hurt leg. 'Did I say thanks for coming back for me, Lex?' he says between pained grimaces. 'Because thanks for coming back for me.'

I frown. 'Just save your energy for mending your leg,' I tell him. 'I hope I haven't made it worse by letting you walk. Your dad'll be really angry with me.'

'Never. I state that emphatically,' George states emphatically. 'My dad thinks you're wonderful.'

'But it's my fault you're hurt! If I hadn't stomped off—'

'Course it isn't. Anyway, you were right to be annoyed with me.'

'Why?' Is he finally going to admit that his crush on

74

Jess is hopeless and, more importantly, potentially irritating to me?

'I . . . I wasn't completely honest with you before. There's something I didn't tell you. I'll tell you now . . . in a minute.'

His eyes look weird. Combined with the strange way he's talking, it makes me wonder if he's delirious. Then I remind myself it's because his eyes are the wrong colour. Still, the way he's talking *is* worrying. I think we need help here.

I jump to my feet. 'First I'm getting Mr Trench. You're acting weird . . . er than usual. I think you really might have broken bones.'

'No, listen, it's important. It's going to sound weird . . . er than usual' – he copies me with a slight smile – 'but I don't know how else to say it. There's something you need to know.'

I turn my next wave of worry into a joke. 'I know everything in the world that I need to know,' I tell him. Well, except what Drew was doing with Gemma just now. But broadly this is a true fact.

George ignores me. 'It's about the game – you know, *Pygmalions*?'

Uh-oh. 'What about it?'

'I . . .' He widens his eyes. 'I think it has powers!'

There he goes. *Delirious!* I ignore the niggle that I've been thinking similar things all morning.

'George, I'm getting you help.'

'But that's just it. I've *got* help. *We've* got help! The game, Lex! Look, I'm going to spell it out.' He makes every word really clear. 'The things. That we're changing. In the game. Are changing. In real life.' He fixes me with his pools of blue. 'I saw your film, Lex. My eyes are a different colour.'

'I was fiddling with the light settings,' I say. But I wasn't – not then.

'Hayden's skin was clearer. Cam's hair was less red. And then there's Matt . . .'

I narrow my eyes. 'What *about* Matt?'

'Didn't you notice his . . . attitude? Also, there's you – you altered something in your Pygma yesterday, didn't you? Something that's actually changed about you.'

I pull at my top. 'No.'

He shakes his head. 'Look, Lex, I know it sounds weird, but it's true. The settings from the game are affecting reality. Dad told me there was a chance the changes weren't working because they hadn't been activated properly, and I really think we managed it yesterday.'

'Was your dad talking about changing things in real life, though, George?' Because if he was, then they're both barking. They should start a company called Barking & Son.

76

'No, no, he meant *in the game*, from when he first tested it. But I really think . . . I think we've got it working, and it's affecting us.'

'George. What you're saying is impossible,' I try, though really I don't have a leg to stand on here. Ahem, kind of like George. 'You can't change the world with a game.' I shake my head slowly to show him how crazy that sounds.

'Not the world. *Us*. We can change things for us. The people we created Pygmas for.'

I open my mouth to launch into a tirade about George's craziness, and I think he knows it because he suddenly goes, 'Ow, ow, my leg! I'm in so much pain, Lex! Please get Mr Trench!'

I give him a look. 'OK, but when you're all sorted out in your traction later, we're going to talk about this. Hang in there, Frodo.'

I leg it back to Base Camp Har Har with a whole different mission on my mind. Now I just want George to be OK. And I don't just mean his leg, either. There's something wrong with his mind if he thinks that settings from the game are coming true.

I hear the low-frequency boom of Trenchie before I see him. He's in the side room by the kitchen area, and I peer through the bubble-glassed window in the door to see who he's shouting at. It's a blurry-looking Matt. He's not just blurry because of the frosted glass – he actually looks wobbly round the edges, and really frowny and grouchy, for him. He's usually Mr Nice Guy, ready with a joke and a laugh. What you see is what you get, with Matt.

The way Mr Trench is standing tall and booming, though . . . Well, if I didn't know better, I'd say Matt was being told off. And sulking about it.

I edge closer, but it's no good, of course – I can't hear what they're saying and I can't see either of their faces clearly enough.

But if Matt's in trouble, it might explain why Gemma wasn't with him just now. Maybe Drew and Matt had to swap places to leave Trenchie free to have a go at Matt. But about what? Matt's acting like a whole different person in there.

It's like someone has changed his attitude to life.

You know, like someone has moved the slider on his *Life* settings as far over to 'negative' as they'll go.

Like I did yesterday when I was trying to prove to George that I wasn't after Matt.

Is this what George was talking about before?

George! I'm the worst friend in the world. George is injured – this is no time to be standing around coming up with improbable reasons for Matt suddenly dipping his toe in uncharacteristic Improver waters.

I knock on the door and the Trench vibrations stop, which I figure is enough of a signal for me to burst in.

Matt stares at me, and I have to re-focus for a second. I'm not even sure he's looked at me since I finished with him – not properly. This is probably the first time. But I have other things to think about.

So I announce George's accident, and Mr Trench pretends to be calm while his eyes dart with panic and the thought of potential claims from angry parents who watch daytime telly and know all about Ambulance Chasers Insurance Ltd.

'Very well. Matthew, kindly wait here while I deal with this emergency, and while I'm gone you can have a THINK about your ATTITUDE.'

Matt makes a face and mouths something rude at Trenchie the minute his back's turned. When I see it, I can't help myself.

I say, 'What's the *matter* with you?' It's not exactly how I pictured the start of our first conversation since the day I broke up with him at school and instantly regretted it.

Not that he seemed all that bothered, as I remember. He wasn't exactly upset at all, not with Gemma waiting in the background.

He looks miserable now, though. He slouches into a chair in the corner of the room, pulling an iPod out of his pocket and plugging in, shutting his ears. Then he shuts his eyes too, and turns away. He's shutting me out. I know this technique – I use it myself all the time, mostly with Mum. Matt's so wrapped up in himself right now that he may as well have a bow on top of his head and a giftcard tucked into his side pocket.

My heart sinks, but I remember George and run out. Mr Trench is frowning by the door, clutching a small red case with a white cross on it and waiting for me to lead him to my injured friend.

George gives a weak smile when he sees us, and our teacher attempts a bit of half-hearted first aid that reminds me of when I used to play nurses with Gemma in Year Two. She was always going on about 'elevating' legs too. After George winces once too often, Mr Trench gives up, puts down the case and says he's going to call an ambulance. George's dad is contacted, and I go with George to hospital because he asks me to.

So that's pretty much the end of the first day of the film course. I can't exactly call it boring after all.

It turns out that George's leg is fine, but he has a broken toe.

It's terrible because I go through a brief stage of finding this hysterically funny. Every time I think about it, I get laughter bubbles in my stomach that threaten to squeeze out of the corners of my mouth. I know that breaking anything is serious stuff, but there's just something about a toe – *one* toe. And it happened when he tripped over what was basically a very large twig. I mean, honestly. George can't even manage to get an *injury* that sounds sexy.

We're at the hospital, and George and his dad are off with the doctors. Meanwhile Mum somehow found out we were here and came to help out because, as she said, tight-lipped, 'Martin has issues with hospitals, as you know.'

Actually, I didn't know – or rather, I don't really remember – but it explains why Martin was shaking like a leaf when he arrived to be there for his son at his time of broken-toed need.

Mum looks at me sternly as another giggle escapes. I mumble something about the toilet and slink outside with my mobile to tell my mates what's happened. Then I stand against the wall and remember that my only real friend is having his toe put in traction, or whatever they're doing in there.

I should text Jess. I mean, she's still a friend, isn't she? Even if she'd rather be friends with a GCSE paper. I bet George would want her to know about this. But my stupid fingers keep bleeping up to the 'Gemma' entry. Like Gemma would even care. And, I realize, this is actually *her* fault and not mine! If she hadn't been under that tree with Drew, I wouldn't have got so annoyed with George and he wouldn't have run after me and tripped.

I bet Gemma would give me some good advice about

Martin's hospital phobia, though. If there's one thing she's always loved, it's taking care of everyone – fixing people and cheering them up. Her favourite game when we were little was Hospitals, and she hasn't really changed. She's always looking for chances to practise her skills – she admits it herself. The worst thing about that is it's exactly how she got together with Matt – she went to 'check he was OK' after I finished with him, and they ended up snogging. Yeah, thanks a lot, friend.

I shiver and look up at the tall hospital tower. It's only October but it's freezing out here. There's a woman in the doorway next to me, cupping her hands over her mouth as she lights a cigarette. I fiddle with my phone's clapper-board charm, which was a present from George on my last birthday. He thought I'd like it, and he was right. George tries so hard. If only I could fancy a George-like boy instead of guys like Matt and Drew. Guys who invariably end up with Gemma. The trouble with the world is that everyone fancies the wrong person. We're all in a love-chain made of broken links.

Oh, this is ridiculous. I decide to text Jess. She's nothing like me – she wouldn't think George's toe injury was remotely funny, even for a second. Maybe she'll feel sorry for him and rush into his arms. I can at least do George a favour after what happened.

Someone appears beside me. 'Lex, there you are!'

It's Martin. He's panting like he's just run round the

building three times. I put my phone back in my pocket. Jess-baiting can wait.

'Your mum was worried.' Puff puff. 'You disappeared. You should have told her.' Puff. 'Where you were going.'

I shrug. I seem to spend half my life telling Mum where I'm going.

He gives me a conspiratorial nudge. 'I did tell her you could take care of yourself.'

Oh, I like Martin. I smile at him. 'How's George?' I wonder if he'd tell me the truth if his son was still acting insane and talking about magical games.

'Not too bad. They're taping his toe and he won't need a cast, but he'll have to keep his weight off it. They're giving him crutches.'

'Really? For one toe?' I knew I'd underestimated this toe thing. I feel really mean and I want to give George a hug now.

'Yes. Won't be long. I told your mum I'd find you because I . . . needed some air.' Martin glances desperately towards the car park, as if he wants to make a run for it.

I go a bit hot and cold as I think about one of the issues Martin probably has with hospitals. George's mum, Martin's wife, died in a car accident. We were only little, and George didn't live next door to us then, but he was already at our school, so his family can't have lived too far away. Maybe this was the hospital they went to. Maybe Mum even saw them that day – it's possible. She doesn't really talk to me about work, and she certainly wouldn't have when I was in Year One. And George never talks about his mother or what happened.

I suddenly feel bad for having stood here feeling sorry for myself and inwardly raging about Gemma, while Martin – and probably George too – have proper bad memories to deal with.

Mum appears at the door with a hobbling George.

'There you are!' She doesn't smile at me. 'I've taken some last-minute annual leave. I thought I'd help George home.'

'I'll do it, Mum!' I rush round to George's side and hold his arm, trying to be the best friend in the world. He nods gratefully in my direction and concentrates on teetering on his crutches.

Mum still isn't smiling as we walk away, despite my total Good Daughter impression. It's probably the effects of being around Martin, though. I wish she'd get over her problems with him. The smoker in the door-way glances at us, and I wonder whether she's seeing us as a family – mum, dad, brother, sister. If only Mum and Martin could sort things out.

Mum ruins this daydream by talking overly politely to Martin on the long walk to the car, her mouth a tense line and her words full of lemon-zest. Then it's shattered completely when our parents' strides leave us behind, and the first thing George says when they're out of earshot is the very un-brotherly, 'I've worked it out. You changed your breasts.'

'What?'

'In the game. Haven't you? I came to that conclusion when they were taping my toe and I needed something to take my mind off it.' He sits down on a nearby bench, leaning his crutches against a recycling bin like he's resting his case.

'Urgh, George! So you thought about *my body*? You're sick!' I perch next to him. 'And anyway, it's nothing to do with the game – it's just that my clothes have got a bit tight, and it's a right pain. And also,' I add quickly so that he doesn't dwell on that, 'who says *breasts* instead of *boobs*?'

'I do. And it's not sick, it's just . . . male.'

'*Sick* male.'

'Don't make me feel bad! It's normal. I read about it.'

I think about the contents of his bookcase. 'In *The Lord of the Rings* or *Harry Potter*?'

He smiles at me as if I understand him, which I so do not. '*Harry Potter*, of course.' He adds pensively, 'Hermione Granger's as gorgeous as Jess.'

'George! You are seriously shocking me right now. You fantasize about fictional characters, don't you?'

'Maybe.'

'Ooh, Hermione Granger . . .' I tease him. 'Wearing only an invisibility cloak!'

He grins. 'God, Lex, don't do this to me! My dad's over there.'

I wave at Martin, who's standing by the car now, looking pained but patient. George calls over to him – something about needing a brief rest.

I give George a firm stare. 'Well, just make sure you don't think like that about *me*, OK? You're—'

'I sincerely hope you weren't going to say I'm like a brother, because as I keep telling you, I'm absolutely not, and our parents don't even like each other so we'll never be step-siblings.' He looks across at them, and he's right. You can totally see the frost between them, and it is not because it's a cold day.

'I was actually going to say that you're disgusting.' I nod self-righteously.

'You're the one who keeps telling me I need to see other girls. Anyway, I'm in love with someone else so you don't have to worry.'

'Oh, I'm not worried about myself. But I'm worried about *you*. You're talking like you've fallen off Planet Normal and you're in orbit in the Weirdy Way.'

'Maybe, but I'm right that you changed your *Looks* settings, aren't I? There was a body-shape selector. You didn't move it far – maybe one notch towards curvy?'

There's a silence.

'Yes,' I admit.

'And I changed my eye colour, and there were the slight inaccuracies in Hayden and Cam's *Looks* settings.'

'And Jess's hair was shinier than usual, which is your fault.' I can't believe I'm talking as if George really *did* make things happen with his game.

'And the biggest one – Matt's *Life* setting.'

Neither of us says anything for a while.

George announces, 'You know, Lex, you should stop pretending to me that you're not in love with Matt. Because I was thinking about that too, and it all makes sense now. I mean, it explains why you're funny with Gemma, and why you've never done anything about Drew even though you go on about fancying him and you're not exactly . . .'

'I'm not exactly *what*?'

'You know.'

I glare at him. 'I don't.'

'You're not exactly *shy*.' I don't think I've ever heard George so outspoken. I wonder what painkillers they gave him in there. 'You know, about asking boys out and . . . stuff.'

'*Stuff*?' Stuff is not a George word. Paraphernalia, accoutrements, chattels – those are George words. What is happening to my friend? He is limping towards the twenty-first century. On crutches.

'I was there when you got together with Matt,' he reminds me. He was too. Matt had one of those birthday parties where the whole school isn't invited to someone's house but turns up anyway. George knew Jess would be there and his dad offered us a lift. I think we'd been there about five minutes when I first did the birthday-kiss thing with Matt, which led to us snogging on and off right up until the minute Matt's parents got home and I legged it with my friends.

I didn't even notice at the time that Gemma was acting weird after we left.

'What's your point?'

'I've seen you in action. So if you really liked Drew, I know you'd have grabbed him by now.'

Well, I think George analysing my love life like this is possibly more excruciating than him checking out my new-look boobs. 'I don't know what you're talking about,' I say. 'And anyway, Drew doesn't even like me.'

'How do you work that out, Lex?'

'He was off with Gemma today!'

'Only because Matt stormed off swearing and Mr Trench heard, so he left Drew with Gemma while he tried to talk some sense into Matt. You know how Mr Trench can't resist an opportunity to rescue his students from the brink of hooliganism.'

Hold on. '*Matt* stormed off swearing?' That's weird. Matt absolutely reserves his swearing for the times he's wrestling Cam and Hayden to the ground at bus stops, in the manner described in the *How to Behave Like a Total Boy* instruction manual. He doesn't do it in front of *teachers*. He's a golden boy as far as they're concerned. It can actually be a bit irritating.

'Apparently.'

'That's not like Matt.'

'No. Someone changed his *Life* settings.' George gives me a look. 'I keep trying to tell you.'

'Wait – how do you even know about this swearing thing?'

He hesitates. 'I heard Gemma talking about it. When you were filming in the trees.'

Oh. 'Why didn't you tell me?'

Martin calls to us, and George says something back to him about coming over in a minute. Then he gives me a sheepish look. 'I was thinking about telling you, honestly. But you got all upset.' He shuffles his foot. 'Then things went a bit wrong for me.'

'So Matt's different *Life* settings are what got him into trouble with Trenchie? And the reason Gemma ended up paired with Drew?' I can't believe I'm saying this, as if what George is saying could really be happening.

'Yes. Don't worry, we can change it back if you like.'

'I think we'd better.' I have to remind myself that it's a coincidence. I didn't alter my ex-boyfriend's personality with a click of the mouse. George just *thinks* I did.

Both scenarios are a bit worrying.

The next thing George says is even more alarming. 'Well, I've decided I'm definitely changing some of the other settings tonight,' he says.

I feel the need to inject some cold, hard reality into this conversation. 'George, nothing you change in the game is going to change anything in real life.' My injection probably isn't very effective because it's laced with doubt.

'OK, so what's the harm?' He looks very serious. 'I'll change some of those *Looks* settings back to normal, like Cam's and Hayden's, before they have one of their rare glances in a mirror and notice it themselves. And I was thinking of making some changes so that Jess wants to be with me.' He gives a thrilled little smile.

I roll my eyes. 'Oh, I knew it! I knew from the start that you were going to do that! I can't believe you waited until now! I'm surprised your Pygmas aren't married already.'

He looks a bit hurt. 'I told you, you need an extra add-on for that. Besides, I don't want to *marry* Jess.'

I raise my eyebrows sceptically, but he continues. 'I'm just talking about some changes ... to make her notice me. I want things to develop naturally. I want a proper relationship, and they go in stages. You know, like the game's settings. *Kiss*, *Date*, *Love*. I think you need the stages to get to the real thing.' He frowns for a second. 'Though shouldn't it be *Date*, then *Kiss* and then *Love*?'

'I'm sure it works in any order.' I think of how things went with Matt. Kiss, date, love ... hate. Get over it. Kiss and date again, and more ... I hope.

'You're probably right. I love Jess already. And you definitely kissed Matt before you went out with him. You ate his face off.'

'George!' There he goes again. 'What's the matter with you? That's the second time you've mentioned that in as many minutes.'

'Well, I've been thinking about it.'

'Well, *stop* thinking about it.'

'I'm pre-programmed to think about it. I read about that too.'

'You're pre-programmed to think about me snogging Matt?'

'No! You know what I mean.'

'I don't.'

'You do. Rhymes with Lex. Apparently teenage boys think about it every seven seconds.'

'Stop stop *stop*! You can't even *say* it!'

'I can think about it, though.'

'Omigod, George, please.' I can't believe him sometimes. He's the strangest friend in the world. 'I do *not* want to know. And anyway, girls think about it too, you know.'

'Really?' His eyes grow huge. '*It*? Girls?'

I nod.

He looks like he's about to fall over in shock, even though we're sitting down. '*All* of them?'

'I should think so.'

He bites his bottom lip. 'I'm going to think about that later.'

'Urgh!' I leap up, shrieking. 'Urgh! Urgh!'

George looks affronted. 'That is *it*, Alexa Murphy! I did *not* mean whatever you're clearly thinking I mean.'

I sit back down, but I say, 'You so did!'

'OK, I am changing the subject! Now!'

'You started it.'

'Even so.' He takes a deep breath. 'So can I change anyone's settings for you? You know – *Kiss*, *Date*, *Love*? Like Drew . . . ?' He looks resigned. 'Or Matt? This is your chance.'

'That's not changing the subject,' I mumble.

I glance around. Martin's giving me a strange look, probably because of my earlier shrieks, and Mum is sending me and George narrow-eyed arrows with messages attached that say *Hurry up!*

'Your dad's waiting for us,' I say, avoiding the question.

We make our way over to Martin's sensible car. George sits in the front because of his foot – or maybe because Mum immediately climbs into the back beside me, avoiding Martin. Nobody says anything much until after Martin has taken a year to park in the residents' bay nearest to our houses and I'm helping George out of the car while the grown-ups do the shuffly, awkward small-talk thing.

Then George mouths at me, a repeat of earlier: *Drew or Matt?*

I hesitate. Then I mouth back, *Matt*, and wait for his protests.

He kind of grimaces but he mouths, *Kiss, Date or Love?* and I hold up three fingers to show I want all three. I want it all.

He says, 'If you're sure that's what you want.'

I nod. 'But change his *Life* settings back first,' I remind him. 'Plus I want longer hair.' I might as well, seeing as this is all crazy anyway.

I think I said that louder than I meant to, because Mum turns and starts having a go at me about the Great Home Hair Extension Disaster and how my bald patch is still clumpy.

This gives Martin time to escape from the clutches of awkwardness and up to his front door, with George shambling along behind him.

'It's never going to work!' I call to George.

'I hope you haven't bought another home kit, Lex,' says Mum, who's now stuck on the subject of hair extensions and clearly thinks I'm discussing them with

George – and doesn't find that weird. Well, she has told me a few times that she thinks George is 'a real character'. And he is, but not in the way *she* means. He just doesn't follow the same Boy Instruction Manual as Matt.

As Martin says goodbye and shuts the door behind them, George does this little half-wave at me, his face full of determination.

There's NO WAY Matt is suddenly going to want to kiss me or date me again, let alone love me. It is impossible to change people using the settings of a game.

This fact doesn't stop me thinking about the possibility all evening. I really want to pop round to see George and find out whether he's made those changes, but when I suggest it to Mum – though I say I want to 'check George is coping OK with his toe' – she goes tight-lipped and says she's had 'quite enough of our neighbours for one day, thank you very much', and anyway, 'that boy needs his rest'.

I think about lying again and saying I'm going to Jess's, but I'm not sure whether Mum would let me do that either. George's brush with that branch seems to have reminded her of her own child's vulnerability and she's being super-attentive tonight, even trying to have proper conversations with me while she's cooking.

She insists on eating tea in the 'dining room' – which is a bit of grand name for what used to be the junk room.

The corners are full of my old toys, stacked messily on Ikea's finest pine-look shelving. But ever since my own, slightly scarier brush with medical emergency, Mum's had this thing about eating here and having Family Time whenever she's home. With those crazy shifts she works, this is not actually very often. I have to admit that it's sort of nice to eat with someone for a change instead of rushing to George's for biscuits and then eating some curly-edged sandwich Mum's left me, like I normally do. The only problem is fielding the questions.

Tonight it's all about yet another youth group she wants me to join, and the film course, and is there anything I want to tell her about my friends?

I can normally work out what she wants to hear and provide her with it, nicely packaged in the perfect words for her approval, but this time I'm not quite sure what she's getting at. I start by agreeing to go to her youth group 'some time' – i.e. never – and telling her what I've learned about cameras and the cosmos – i.e. not very much, but enough to be kind of enjoying myself. And my friends are all fine.

'That's good, Lex,' she says, though her eyes say, *That's not what I meant*. Then she adds, 'I'm glad the course is going well. Your teacher thought you needed a creative outlet. He says you're' – she sits up in a pompous, Trench-like way – '*very talented in the visual arena*. He wants to build your confidence.'

95

Oh yes. Mr Trench gushed praise at me for about a month last time I got an A at school, even though it was in some timewaster of a lesson – the kind of thing you do at the end of the school year when the teachers want to torture you for a few more hours before setting you free. I painted a mural of our local high street. It was really simple: I stuck ten pieces of paper together and painted the same scene on each one, with tiny changes, like pressing PAUSE and FAST-FORWARD really slowly on a DVD. Or like a very short film reel. All the teachers went mad over it and I got a bit suspicious that they weren't saying *Ooh, look at the artistic talent in this one*, but more *Ooh, let's be nice to the failing girl for a bit of a change from our boring teacher routine*.

I communicate this to Mum with a look and she gets it straight away. I love those rare moments when she's on my side.

'Don't worry, I told him you were very talented in *plenty* of arenas,' she says. 'So, Lex . . . is everything OK between you and your friends?'

There's that question again. What does she want to hear?

'It's fine,' I say, which definitely isn't it, because then she says, 'OK. Help me wash up?'

Oh no! Prolonged chat under the guise of household chores! She's been watching *Supernanny for Teens* again, or whatever those programmes are called – the ones that

96

tell parents how to 'deal with troublesome adolescents'. *Have a quiet word with your teen*, they always recommend. *Try to get them to help you so that they feel useful as they open up to you.* I so hope she's not going to send me to Brat Camp next. Although, in a way, she already has, with this film course. After all, Gemma's on it, and she's a complete brat.

My thoughts turn to Gemma. I consider George's explanation of why Gemma was with Drew in the forest. I wonder what got into Matt today. I need to spend more time thinking about what's going on with my friends, and less time working out what exactly Mum wants me to tell her.

'I'll wash up by myself, Mum,' I offer, and she nearly dies on the spot. She'd check her hearing aid if she had one. 'Isn't your favourite plastic surgery thing on again tonight?' I add quickly, to distract her. '*Boob Jobs from Hell*, or whatever it's called?'

She laughs and gives me a hug. 'It's about all kinds of reconstructive surgery, Lex. You should watch it with me . . . when you've finished.'

Then she steps back and looks at me, her eyes full of pride at my chore-offering goodness, with a touch of *my little girl is growing up*. Eek – I hope she hasn't noticed my magical breast enhancement.

'Come and talk to me afterwards, OK?' she insists.

But by the time I've washed up, she's so clearly

absorbed in the world of plastic body parts that I can sneak off upstairs instead to chat to George online.

He's not there, and he doesn't reply to the three texts I send him either, and this goes on for the rest of the evening. It's driving me crazy.

I have trouble sleeping because I keep thinking about the game and how it must take hours to work, because the changes definitely didn't happen instantly. But how *many* hours – does George know? Did he remember to change my hair like I asked him to and, if so, at what point will I suddenly sprout the perfect hair extensions? Will I feel it happening? I touch my hair but it feels the same – tufty in places, and too short. I pull it over my ears out of habit, even though there's no one around to see.

And at what point will Matt want to kiss me again? How will *that* feel? I dwell on it for a long time.

Eventually I fall into a fitful kind of sleep where I dream about Matt. I go to kiss him but he turns round and he has this really long hair, though his ears stick out of it at the sides and they're ultra-massive, joke ears. When I laugh, he gets all offended and walks off with Gemma, who has appeared from behind a tree with Drew. And then Drew scoops me into his arms and is about to kiss me when George appears on horseback waving a sword at him – and I wake up with a start, my alarm clock shaking my bedside table so much that it almost knocks my mobile onto the floor.

I pick the phone up from where it's teetering and immediately notice I have six new messages, and it's not even seven o'clock.

The first is from George, last night. I can't believe I missed the alert, but it must have been just after I fell asleep. It says: `Made changes!!! Thank me later.`

There's one from Jess, saying she's planning on getting to the course early and she'll see me soon. That girl is way too keen.

The next four – count 'em – *four* are from a number I deleted months ago, after Gemma told me the thing that made me finish with Matt. The thing I now suspect she completely made up so that she could sideline me and get together with Matt herself. It was a clever plan she hatched, making me totally look like the bad guy if you didn't know what was behind it, which no one really knows except Gemma because I was too ashamed to tell anyone – even George. Proper *evil*.

So, yeah, the number is Matt's. I've been thinking lately that I never actually heard Matt's side of what Gemma reported. I took her word for it, and I stormed up to him and finished with him and deleted his number from my phone, and then Gemma was there. *Checking that Matt was OK*, as she put it. Snogging him that same day, as far as I can tell. And since that day he's barely even looked at me, so who *knows* what she's told him about me.

I've kept all this to myself, anyway. You become an expert at living in your own little world when you're me. Lex-land, population: 1.

But I let Matt in a while ago, before I threw him out.

And now he's suddenly texting me again, saying he wants to see me.

What's going on?

Whatever it is, it feels magic.

`Meet me?` Matt says in the first one, from about two hours ago. Then, `Please meet me?` an hour ago, and then, `Lex need 2 see u.` And lastly: `Am here.`

Here?

I instinctively leap out of bed and reach for my hairbrush, though he can't really mean *here*. But before I can even glance in the mirror, Mum appears in the doorway, all ready for work and wearing her morning expression, which combines clean-uniformed efficiency with sleepy-eyed daze. Mum is not a morning person – in fact, she used to work nights and I'd have sleepovers at George's, until my health scare. Now Mum works long day shifts, which is why I get loads of afternoons and early evenings to myself. Mum says it's better that way but she doesn't smile when she says it.

'*Matt* is here,' she tells me now. 'Downstairs. He says he wants to see you.' She gives me a curious look, but she doesn't seem annoyed. Matt has the ability to totally charm parents, even when he turns up on the doorstep first thing in the morning.

'Are you back together, Lex?' Mum asks, pretend-casually. She yawns and rubs her eyes.

I don't tell Mum many details about my life, or not as many as she asks for, anyway, but she knows I was going out with Matt for a while, and then I wasn't. She met him a couple of times when he came over to see me. Once she asked me about him when I was in a good mood, fizzing with post-date happiness, so I talked a bit more than usual. Among other things, I said, 'Matt's just a completely normal guy, Mum, and he makes me feel normal,' and she laughed and said, 'You *are* normal, Lex . . . but be extra-careful,' which was a mixed message if ever I heard one.

I pause mid-brush because something's weird – I mean, as well as the weirdness of Matt turning up at my house at 7 a.m. The brush isn't reaching the end of my hair when I expect it to. What's going on? I peer in the mirror.

My hair!

It's *longer*!

'Yay for George,' I mumble, running my fingers through the faraway ends of my hair. Ooh!

Mum seems to notice at about the same time I do, though hopefully she hasn't heard my George comment.

She gives me a long sleep-glazed look. 'Is that why you crept away last night?' she sighs. 'Lex, I told you those home kits are a waste of money – you don't need them anyway. Shorter hair suits you.' She frowns. 'Though it does look like it worked this time.' Her worry creases deepen. 'Wait – where did you get the money for that kit? It looks like a really good one. It must have cost a lot and . . .' Her eyes darken. 'Please don't tell me you got George to pay!'

Oh no. So she *did* hear me.

'Lex, the Richardses are our neighbours, and obviously we should be courteous, and I know it's convenient to occasionally get lifts from *that man*, but we should be careful about accepting too many favours from them. It's not right. I think you spend far too much time with that boy as it is . . .'

Matt is downstairs so I don't really want to argue with her about this now, but I do manage a feeble: 'George is my friend.'

'Yes, OK. You're at school together so it's inevitable, I suppose. And I know he's . . . *you know*, so it's not that I'm worried about *that* side of things, but I just think you need to spend time with some other friends, so in a way I'm glad that Matt is—'

Well, I can't not interrupt *this*. 'Mum, you don't know what you're talking about! Not that it even matters at all, but George isn't "*you know*" ' – I decide not to take the sceptical look off her face with reports of his recent boob-perving, girl-obsessed ways – 'and I have plenty of other friends.' I shake back my wonderful new mane pointedly, because people who have hair like this in shampoo adverts definitely have tons of friends.

'Oh, really? Well, I was talking to Sarah Hartford yesterday.' Her face tightens. She really doesn't like Jess's mum. 'She said that Jess barely sees anyone out of school these days. She's always in her room studying, on her own.'

'It's not my fault if Jess loves her schoolwork so much,' I say. 'Do you know she's even stopped her dance classes?' I add, to support my case.

Mum doesn't veer off-track. 'It's your fault if you text me to say you're with Jess and then I find out you clearly haven't been,' she retorts, which shuts me right up. My mum is fantastic at discipline – it must be her nursely training. She does an amazing line in quiet disappointment that makes you want to throw yourself at her feet and beg for forgiveness. 'You were with George and not Jess, weren't you?'

I wonder for a second whether it would be better to deny it and make up some outrageous thing I was out doing instead, involving criminal activity or worrisome underage stuff. That'd teach her for not wanting me to spend innocent time with my nerdy friend next door. But then I just nod. Which is just as well, because the next thing Mum says is, 'Martin told me in the waiting room.'

Oh. So this is what yesterday's questions were about.

Her eyes go firm. 'I was going to wait until I could have a proper chat to you about this, but since we're here . . . Lex, please don't ever lie to me again.'

The disappointed silence that follows is unbearable. Every bone in my body wants to do the throwing-self-at-her-feet thing.

I restrain myself. 'Sorry,' I mumble.

She picks up steam. 'And I heard that you're not very friendly to Gemma these days either.'

Now I regret never telling Mum anything. I should have known she'd be getting gossip from work, and I should have got in there with my version of events first.

I have to make her see my side. 'That's because of what happened with—' I pause because there's someone else in my doorway. Mum turns sharply.

'Matt!' we both say at the same time.

'I'm sorry, Lex's mum,' Matt says with his characteristic confidence, edged with something else. 'I couldn't wait another minute. I had to see her.' His eyes land on me. 'Lex!'

He strides forward and attempts to sweep me passionately into his arms, like some oily-chested, open-floaty-shirted hero off a romantic novel cover – though he's wearing a football top with three lions on it and no ruffles at all. But that doesn't change the fact that I'm still standing in my bedroom in my scruffy pyjamas and I haven't brushed my teeth and I've barely combed my new-look hair, so when he attempts the arm-sweep thing, I jump away from him and he stumbles.

Mum just stands there, staring.

I gulp as Matt steadies himself and gazes into my eyes.

I know that expression. It reminds me of the look on George's face when he goes on about Jess. But actually I've never seen Matt – or anyone – look at *me* that way before.

'Oh, Lex, I've missed you,' he announces – words I've been longing for him to say. Though I imagined them without . . . that edge. 'I couldn't wait to see you this morning!'

It's kind of . . . desperation.

It's slightly pathetic.

But still. It's Matt, talking to me again. And looking like . . . Well, looking like he wants to kiss me.

He leans in and I shift again without really meaning to. So his kiss lands on my cheek, which actually is just as well, as I don't exactly want him snogging me in front of my mum. Not that Matt seems to care. He just moves and leans in again, and this time I have to step right away. It's a strange thing to do because I've been dreaming of this moment for months. It's just that, oddly enough, my mother was never in a single one of those dreams.

'Will you go out with me again, Lex? Now?'

'*Now?*' I echo, stunned. I've never heard of a date at seven in the morning on a day that's practically a school day. Or on any day, in fact.

'Well, I can't do it *right* now,' Matt says seriously.

'Probably just as well,' I joke. 'With my mum here and all.'

Mum shakes her head in disbelief.

Matt doesn't laugh. He has that look in his eye again. 'I can't make tonight, either! I wish I could. How about tomorrow night?'

'Um . . . but what about Gemma?' I blurt, for some strange reason.

He looks confused. 'Gemma? No, I want to go out with *you*.'

'Oh.' That's so weird. 'OK.'

Then Mum comes alive and throws Matt out of the house with some kind-but-firm words. She tells me she has to go to work and she'll speak to *me* later.

It's only when I pull on the top I've chosen for today that I realize my, ahem, *size* has gone back to normal. Well, normal for me.

I will quite possibly kill George as soon as I see him.

PART TWO:

date

I'm dying to kill George, as well as tell him what happened with Matt – and with my hair – but I only manage a bit of quick hair-flipping before his extra-fussing dad gets him settled in the front seat and turns on the sound system all the way to Base Camp Har Har. The speakers are in the back and it's obvious from Martin's head movements that he's on some kind of naff-metal-from-his-youth nostalgia trip so there's no chance of conversation with George, even if we could talk about this in front of his dad.

By the time we reach the forest I'm all fluttery-stomached with nerves. I've also managed to forgive George for what he did to my body shape. After all, my clothes fit now and my long hair looks ace. Yesterday my new body shape felt a bit unnatural and uncomfort-able, but now I'm myself again, only with added confidence.

I wave goodbye to Martin, and George starts to

hobble slowly down the path beside me. Yeah, never mind the boob thing. Matt tried to kiss me! And kind of succeeded – as much as I'd want him to with Mum in the room! And I'm going to see him on the course today, and we're likely to get sent out into the wilds to film again, and maybe we'll be paired differently now, and anything could happen. Anything! And I'm going out with him again, and it was effortless! This is fantastic!

I have this niggle about Gemma, though. I sort of hope she's OK, a feeling which takes me by surprise. I'm sure she didn't think twice about me when things were the other way around.

It takes us ages to reach the hut. George stops a lot, partly because he's still getting the hang of his crutches, but mostly because I keep making him stop so that I can properly gauge his reaction to what I'm telling him about Matt. I don't care if we're late.

'Matt wanted to kiss me!' I announce. 'I didn't exactly let him, but he wanted to! And he asked me out!'

'That's great,' George says without much enthusiasm.

'It is!' Well, I'm excited about it, even if my friend's being a misery-guts. 'What's the matter with you?'

He sighs. 'I'm probably just tired.'

I frown at him. 'I hope it's not because you spent ages changing my – you know, *certain* settings.'

'Lex! It took one second. It was just the body-shape

selector, and I thought you'd thank me. You were moaning about your clothes not fitting yesterday.'

'Hmm.' I think that's enough of that. 'So why are you so tired?'

'Dad made me have an early night.'

'Oh yeah, that sounds tiring. Sleep's sooo exhausting.' I yawn just to underline my point.

'He kept checking up on me, making sure I was properly resting,' he explains. 'It meant I couldn't get on the computer for ages.'

'I know! I was messaging you!'

'I thought you might be. But when I finally got on, I was in a rush to get to the game.'

I make a face. 'Oh, thanks a *lot*. The game's more important than me, huh?'

'No, I . . .' George's eyes shadow with guilt and I notice something.

'Hey, you changed your eyes back. Oh, and I was joking, by the way.'

He looks relieved. 'Oh. Yeah, I was using my eye colour as a sort of tester. I was trying to find the moment when . . . things changed in the game.' He leaves a dramatic pause. 'The changes seem to kick in at exactly midnight.'

'Seriously? How can you be sure?'

'I looked in the mirror. A lot. Every ten minutes or so, until my eyes changed.' He yawns, but it's definitely for

111

show. I bet George often stays up geeking at his computer all night.

I think back to the afternoon before the course. 'So that means our first lot of changes happened at midnight, but we didn't notice them until the morning?'

He averts his eyes from my back-to-normal boobs. 'It's a highly qualified guess, yes,' he says. 'I think you can make as many changes as you like throughout the day, but it all takes effect at midnight. I'm glad I figured it out.'

I narrow my eyes at him. 'You read the instruction manual, didn't you, George?'

'Of course not! You know I don't do instruction manuals!' George absolutely prides himself on that. 'Besides, there isn't one. I asked Dad, and we looked everywhere.'

'Ha – you looked for it! So I'm sort of right!' I pretend to be holding pom-poms and do a quick cheer.

George ignores me. 'Anyway, it's a long time to wait for changes to take effect. No wonder Dad says it's total game fail.'

'*Total game fail?*' I mimic. 'Did your *dad* say that?'

'No. You know what I mean.'

I shake my invisible pom-poms at him. 'Get *you*, former old-fashioned boy! You're, like, suddenly *made* of epic win!'

George waves me away. He is zero fun. 'I also checked

to see when the game expires, and it's Friday at midday. A month from when Dad first activated it. After that, it's dead without a new key code, which we don't have.'

I give him a look. 'Meaning, please, Professor.'

'No more game after Friday.'

'OK,' I say. 'So we just have to make the most of it, yeah?' I'm still excited about it. Friday's ages away and I'm back with Matt *now*!

'Yeah, I suppose so.' George frowns. 'What I can't work out, though—'

'Oh, you mean it wasn't in the manual?' I hold my invisible pom-poms in the air in a flamboyant finish.

'I told you there wasn't a manual. What I *can't* work out, though, is why the changes only started happening after that Sunday with you. I swear before that things weren't changing in the game, not even the next day. It seemed completely broken. I wonder if it was something to do with the extended profiles we filled in. Maybe we triggered something on Sunday—'

'Or perhaps it's because *I* was there,' I suggest. 'And I have magical powers.'

George gives me a withering look. 'I think it's something to do with the extended profiles we filled in,' he repeats. 'Not that it's any weirder than you having magical powers.' His crutch 'accidentally' taps me on the leg. 'Lex, do you really think it's working?'

'Yup, Professor Richards, it sure seems to be.'

113

'But it's impossible!' He wobbles in stunned amazement.

I clutch his arm to steady him. 'I know.' Last week, Matt wouldn't even look at me. Today he turns up in my bedroom wanting to kiss me. I have a short daydream about Matt before stopping George again to ask him, 'So did you change Jess's *Love* settings?' How weird would it be if something actually *did* happen between Jess and George now? I can't imagine it. Although she can't have done a Matt. For one thing, she texted me to say that she was getting here early. For another, George would have told me by now, probably a few times. 'Did you set Jess's profile so that she wants to kiss you, date you, love you, or all three?'

'Um, not exactly.' His mouth twitches nervously.

I narrow my eyes. 'What do you mean, not *exactly*?'

'Like I was saying yesterday . . . I want her to *want* to be with me.'

'Well, she will if you change her settings.' It's getting so that this doesn't even sound weird any more. It's amazing how quickly you get used to changes – welcome changes, anyway. 'Matt wanted to kiss *me*. He even asked me out. We reached two settings at once. Next stop: love!' I beam.

'I know, but that's different. You were together before. He probably never *stopped* wanting to kiss you or—'

I hold up a hand to shut him up. 'No, he definitely

114

stopped. He barely even looked at me any more after I dumped him. He ran off with Gemma first chance he got.'

'After *you* dumped *him*, Lex. I'm just saying . . .'

'What *are* you saying? And what have you done about Jess?'

'I'm saying Matt's always liked you that way, if he has any sense. And about Jess . . . I made some other changes instead.' George gives me a guilty look. 'You know how you said I should get other girls interested in me? To show her what she's missing?'

I clutch his arm. 'George, what did you do? Whose settings have you changed?'

He mumbles the next thing with his head turned away, and I have to ask him to repeat it. Twice. Eventually I get: 'Every girl on the course.'

'Every girl on the COURSE!'

'Ssh.'

'No, I won't shush! Every GIRL on the COURSE! George! What, even me?' I examine my feelings for George, but they don't seem to have changed, thankfully. He's still my annoying friend-type person. *Extremely* annoying.

'No, except you, because you freak out whenever I suggest that I've noticed you're female. And Jess, obviously, since that's the whole point. I want her to be jealous.'

115

I let his comment about me ride because we have other things to consider. 'So Lia, Tia and Kathryn,' I think aloud. 'And Gemma? Omigod, Gemma?'

He nods.

I can't think about that. 'And Ms Cosgrove?'

'Don't be ridiculous!' He pauses. 'We didn't make an avatar for her.'

'George!'

'It was a joke.'

'Maybe, but it doesn't change the fact that you've gone crazy! One day of having the power to make people fancy you, and it's gone right to your head, mad professor boy!'

He looks sulky. 'Well, you're the same. You asked me to change Matt's settings for you and you're over the moon with the results.' He replaces the sulkiness with guilt. 'Though I should probably tell you . . . I didn't only change Matt's settings. For you, I mean.'

Uh-oh. 'What are you talking about?'

He doesn't meet my eye but he doesn't turn away either. 'I've set Drew to want to kiss you and date you too.'

'What?' *What?* 'Why?' I think I might hyperventilate. I don't know what to say. I manage, 'George!'

He puts on an innocent face. 'It seemed like the right thing to do. And won't it be like what you suggested for me and Jess? Matt will want you more if Drew wants you too, no?'

I brush away the fact that I might have been thinking the same thing recently. 'No! It's just going to cause problems!' I eye him suspiciously. 'And you've only done this because you don't want me to get back with Matt, haven't you?'

'But it gives you options,' George protests. 'Don't you think? In case you decide Matt's not right for you. And Drew is.'

Oh, I'm so right! He still doesn't approve of me seeing Matt, so he's stirring things up for me. 'Matt *is* right for me! Change Drew's settings, George! Change them now! I can't have Drew after me when I'm just getting back with Matt!' Especially not when my feelings for Drew aren't entirely platonic, if I'm honest.

'I can't! Not until we get home, and then the change won't take effect until midnight.'

Thinking about Drew brings back all the confusion that left me when Matt tried to kiss me this morning. I get extra butterflies at the thought of *Drew* trying to kiss me, for a start. I'm also a bit relieved that nothing is likely to happen between Drew and Gemma now, after my suspicions yesterday – even though George's explanation of why Gemma ended up paired with Drew seems right. But this isn't what I wanted. I wanted Matt again, without complications!

'Just see how it goes,' George suggests.

'You're ruining my life with that game!' I tell him.

His back-to-normal eyes flare. 'I'm just trying to *help*! Like you helped me with the Jess thing. And *ssh* – Lia and Tia will hear you!'

We're nearly at the hut now and the Flirt Twins are standing in the doorway. I don't think they could have heard us but they've definitely seen George. They're at his side like a shot, giggling as their faces fill with sympathy for his injury.

George smiles at them pathetically, then at me triumphantly, and disappears into Base Camp Har Har.

Inside the hut, things go completely wild.

George and I are slightly late, and Lia and Tia inform us that the teachers are in the side room preparing for the next session, and we're all just supposed to get on with what we were doing yesterday. This is something George and I have no idea about, seeing as we were at the hospital all afternoon. But Lia and Tia are keen to fill us in – well, George, anyway. As far as I can see, it seems to involve a lot of hanging around near George, pointing at his toe and giggling.

Lia and Tia are soon joined by Gemma, who is striding about pulling up chairs and generally making a huge fuss of George. She goes into her full nurse mode, elevating his leg and stroking his arm. Oh, actually it's her flirt mode. It's completely Gemma, though. It is so strange to see her like this with a boy who isn't Matt.

118

'Gemma, where's Matt?' I ask before I think about what a completely stupid thing this is to be asking her. Does she know I'm in the process of stealing her boyfriend? Stealing him *back*, I mean – he was mine first. In any case, however crazy she is about George right now, thanks to the game . . . surely she'll mind? I don't want to be as bad as her! I haven't thought this through at all.

Gemma frowns at me and looks confused for a second. 'My Matt?' she says. Then her face changes and her eyes harden like she's under some kind of spell. 'Don't know, don't care.' She laughs and turns back to George. 'Can I do anything to make you more comfortable, babe?'

I roll my eyes and glance around, but there's definitely no sign of Matt. Or Drew, which is less surprising, what with him being Mr Non-Attender. I'm shocked about Matt, though. I would have thought he'd be dying to see me. I realize that sounds completely big-headed, but then I did experience his new-found keenness this morning.

George doesn't know what to make of all the sudden female attention. He keeps giving me little thrilled smiles and casting nervous glances in the direction of Jess and Kathryn, who are sitting with piles of paper on their lap and sketching pictures in large squares. I work out from what I know of film-making that they're storyboarding – drawing scenes from the plot onto plain paper to use as a kind of plan of their script. Great – that must be what George and I missed. I really wanted to hear about that too. And it's not as if I wasn't already lost enough on this course, in my usual Improver way.

After a few minutes Kathryn joins the other girls at George's side, explaining things shyly and showing him some sketches, mumbling so much that I can't really make out what she's saying, even though she keeps looking up and smiling at me too, trying to include me. She seems all right, really, though obviously into George. Like every girl here except me and Jess.

I go over to say hi to Jess, but she barely looks up from her paperwork so I bet she hasn't even noticed that George is suddenly the most popular boy in the room. I think there's a flaw in George's plan after all. Jess is so single-minded about anything study-related that she doesn't ease up for a second.

I watch her for a bit, wondering whether George should change her *Life* settings instead of every other girl's *Love* settings. Maybe he could make Jess more easy-going and carefree. It could be more important than any number of flirting females.

I glance back at George. He and Kathryn are laughing together now, and Gemma, Lia and Tia look like they want to scratch her eyes out.

Jess taps me on the shoulder. 'Hey, I've been trying to talk to you.'

'Oh, sorry. I thought you were too busy.' I manage to stop myself adding 'for me', because it sounds a bit pathetic, though I really do miss Jess since she went on this total study kick.

'Yeah, it's just . . .' She holds her paper out to me and frowns. 'Can you help me, Lex? This is for the final show already – we had to get started yesterday. There's so little time! You always have the best ideas. And by the way, I love the hair extensions.'

I smile at her. Jess has always gone out of her way to make me feel good about myself, even when she knows how much I struggle with school stuff. Maybe I really should go and study with her some time, except that Mum probably won't believe me now if I say that's what I'm doing. I'd probably need a signed note from Jess's mum and photographic evidence of my arrival at the Hartford residence.

Speaking of Jess's mum, who's also Drew's aunt . . . 'Has Drew overslept again?' I ask casually, even though I'm back with Matt now.

I'm just interested. That's all.

Jess does her usual Drew-induced eye-roll. 'Yes. *Again* is right. Mum's driving him here later.' She gives me a look, hesitates for a second and then says, 'Lex, you know . . . this isn't the first time you've asked me about

121

Drew. Plus I saw the way you talked to each other yesterday. Can I just ask . . . Are you actually *interested* in my loser step-cousin?'

Wow, Jess has finally noticed something about me! Though not a good thing. 'No! No! He's not a loser!' Oops. 'I mean, no, I'm not! In fact, I'm seeing Matt again.'

She nearly drops her neat storyboarding in shock. 'When did that happen? What about Gemma? I thought those two were crazy in love.'

I shrug in the direction of Gemma, who is still fawning over George, together with the rest of the female film course population. Jess follows my gaze, so she should finally see what a popular boy George is. Will it make her realize that he could be the boy of her dreams?

'I don't believe you lot,' she remarks, her eyes skating right over the George scene and back to me. 'I mean, no offence, Lex, but I thought you and Matt were over months ago. Plus Gemma seemed really into him. Who dumped who this time? Is Gemma OK with this?'

Um. 'Technically, I was with Matt first, you know,' I remind her.

'Yeah, and so were half the other girls in Year Ten and Eleven.' She sits up Jess-ishly straight. 'I'm so glad I'm not involved in any of these secondary school trysts. Boys of our age are incredibly immature – they trample all over girls' feelings. There's so much more to life.' Jess looks at my face and her expression softens. 'I'm not having a go at you, Lex, honest. I just don't want you or Gemma getting hurt. It's *boys* who are the problem. They need to grow up.'

'It's OK. You're probably right.' She probably is.

She bites her lip. 'Anyway, look, Kathryn and I want to end our film with a chase scene. What do you think of this bit . . . ? Would it work if . . . ?' She points to her notes and I try to concentrate on them as much as she does.

Honestly, though, as long as Jess is this serious, George will need to turn into a GCSE paper for her to take any kind of notice of him. I'm definitely mentioning my new idea to him later. I'm sure a more fun-loving, carefree Jess would change her mind about 'secondary school trysts'.

Just as I think that, Drew walks in – super-late and super-gorgeous, making my heart leap. I wouldn't mind a tryst with him, that's for sure.

Though I'm actually supposed to be trysting away with Matt. Who isn't here. Where is he? And why am I always waiting for some boy to arrive?

So then I go right back to thinking that Jess is right. I need to be more like her, not the other way round.

I stare at the piece of paper she's holding, and I ignore the fact that Drew is walking over. I'm so focused on Jess's work that I don't even notice him stop right next to me. And I'm being so helpful to Jess that there's no way I know that Drew is looking at me.

OK, that's not true. I am fully aware of every single movement Drew has made since he walked into the room.

Also, it's not just that he's looking at me. It's the *way* he's looking at me. Like I'm the most fascinating person he's ever met.

This isn't real, though! It's because of the game settings.

Argh!

'Hey, Lex,' he says, and my eyes are drawn to his lovely mouth. 'And Jess.'

Jess rolls her eyes, the way she always does in the presence of Drew.

He focuses on me. 'Mr Trench called me in to see him when I arrived. He said he's changing things around a bit. So I'm with you today, and I'm supposed to bring you up to date with what we did yesterday. By the way, I like your hair.'

He smiles that lovely smile of his.

'You're with *me* today?' I'm suspicious. Did Drew *ask* to be paired with me? I know by now that the computer game makes people do unsubtle things like fawn over George (every girl in this room except me and Jess) and appear in my bedroom first thing in the morning (Matt).

'I think it's because your boyfriend broke his leg,

so he has to stay indoors, and Mr Trench said—'

Oh my GOD! 'George hurt his toe! One toe! And he isn't my boyfriend!'

I look at Jess for confirmation but she's sketching away again now, frowning with the effort of blanking out her annoying cousin.

Drew says, 'Oh, OK. Sorry, I wasn't sure. It's just that I saw you out together the other night at the Bijou and then you told me he was your partner—'

'Not that sort of partner. *You* were at the Bijou?' Did he have a night off from his usual wild partying?

'Yeah.' He grins. 'Is that so surprising?'

'Well, yeah.' Because you're supposed to be out doing bad-boy things. 'Because no one but me and George – my *friend* George – ever goes to the Bijou. Well, unless Mike the Manager holds a special event. You know, like ours this week.'

'I wondered about that,' Drew says. 'It was so quiet. Won't it shut down if it goes on like that?'

'I don't know. It's always been like that.' Oh no, what a horrible thought. 'I hope not.'

'I liked it there. I had to leave early because I didn't realize the film was going to be so long, and I had' – he glances at Jess – 'a thing I had to do.'

That's more like it. He couldn't admit it in front of Jess, so it was probably some kind of gang warfare, or whatever guys like him do all night. I imagine him emerging from the shadows of a pile of burning tyres, looking shady and hot. I dwell on it a bit.

'I missed the end of the film,' he says, interrupting my daydream, 'so I'm going to go again another night, I think . . .' He looks away, as if he's suddenly seen something interesting on the other side of the room.

I'm so busy following his gaze – to the poster that says RESPECT YOURSELF – that I nearly miss what he says next. But not quite.

'. . . go with me?' he says. 'If you felt like seeing it again, I mean? Or whatever else is on. Maybe. Or not.'

Jess looks up for a second before she goes back to sketching, pressing extra-hard with her pen.

Oh no.

Meanwhile my heart is galloping, which is annoying.

'What?' I say, stalling for time. Because I'm pretty sure Drew has asked me out, just when I've finally got back with Matt.

'Um,' Drew says, like he has to gear himself up to say it all over again. It's extremely cute, how shy he's acting, but it has to be an act – I've got to know him since he started at our school, and I remember him at the Jess-family wedding, and he is *not* shy. Shy is the last word you'd use to describe him. You could go through the whole dictionary first. He is more 'aardvark' or 'zebra' than he is 'shy'.

So this has to be strange, game-induced behaviour.

I can't believe George is trying to mess up my romantic reunion with Matt! Not to mention getting me into Jess's bad books.

I shoot George some daggers, which he doesn't see because Lia is now sitting on the knee of his good leg – ugh! – and then I say to Drew, 'But you must have seen those *Lord of the Rings* movies before? They're ancient!'

'I . . .'

'Or at least you must have read the book!' I'm sort of wishing I would shut up, but my mouth keeps going. 'Everyone's read the book. Especially boys!'

Drew goes a bit red. 'I haven't,' he mumbles, plus something else that's lost in mumble-land. I make out the final words. 'Never mind.'

After that, things go mega-awkward between us, and the fact that I keep glancing at the door and wondering why Matt isn't here probably doesn't help.

I never thought I'd say it, but I'm actually happy when Mr Trench and Ms Cosgrove emerge from the side room and start making another one of their everlasting speeches about what we're going to do today. This time I really try to focus as they talk about gathering footage, and how, owing to time constraints, today is the day when we'll get most of our material together, so we'll be out filming for hours to give us time to edit and render the film . . . and ooh, a wasp has flown in, and it's kind of late in the season for wasps, though it does look pretty tired and like it's about to keel over and it will keep bashing itself stupidly against the window and— Oh no, I've drifted off again. Why is everyone except me standing up now?

I scramble to my feet and cast a panicky glance at George, but Gemma has him locked in conversation, so then I look for Jess, but she's halfway out of the door with Kathryn.

I'm about to swallow my pride and tell the teachers that I don't know what I'm supposed to be doing when Drew taps my shoulder.

'Hey, Lex,' he says. 'So, you ready, partner?' His smile says, *No hard feelings*, and makes me feel a bit guilty.

'Were you serious about that?'

'Yes. Why wouldn't I be?'

'I mean, did Mr Trench really tell you to be my partner and stuff, or did you just want to . . .' I can't really finish that sentence without sounding truly big-headed, unless I mention the game, in which case I'll sound insane.

At that point Mr Trench himself appears in front of me. 'Ah yes, Alexa,' he booms mildly. 'Seeing as your former partner is going to be confined to base, probably for the duration of the course, you'll be with Andrew and Gemma for the rest of the week.'

'And *Gemma*?' I say in undisguised horror. She's not listening anyway – she's still leering at George.

'Yeah.' Drew shrugs apologetically. 'Matt got kicked off the course yesterday so I've been working with Gemma.'

Oh yeah. Yesterday.

Wait. 'Matt was kicked off the course?'

'Absolutely not,' Mr Trench emphasizes. 'He was merely told to go home and attend to a family situation that was obviously distressing him, judging by his – ahem – *behaviour*.'

'You should have heard him yesterday, Lex,' Drew adds. 'He was acting like a right—'

'Yes, thank you, Andrew,' says Mr Trench. 'That'll do.'

Drew catches my eye and his expression tells me what he was about to say, which makes me want to laugh.

But I remind myself that this isn't funny. I'm back with Matt now, after all. And a *family situation*? Matt has a perfect shiny family who never get into 'situations', unless it's Matt winning too many football trophies to fit on the mantelpiece next to his twin sister Chloe's dance awards. What's going on, and why don't I know anything about it?

And if something bad's going on at home, what's he doing turning up at my house this morning and asking me out?

And is it my fault – not to mention George's – that he's off the course? Because we changed his *Life* settings and made him lose it?

I start to feel really uncomfortable about the whole thing.

Gemma walks over.

I bet *she* knows what's going on with Matt. Those two are so close. *Were* so close. Matt must have dumped her to get back together with me. My head floods with an odd sort of guilt, even though she deserves this for what she did to me. Still, I find myself wanting to make sure she's OK, or maybe even apologize. I bite my lip. 'Gemma . . .' I start. I have no idea what to say next.

Gemma doesn't even seem to hear me. She smiles sweetly at our teacher. 'Oh, Mr Trench, please can I stay here with George? He might need me! I can help him with . . . things.'

'No, can *I* stay?' says Tia from behind her.

'No, me!' Lia says. 'George needs *my* help.'

Lia and Tia glare at each other. If the Flirt Twins stop being friends over this, I will feel so guilty I'll never touch a computer again.

Before Mr Trench can boom all the girls into the forest, Ms Cosgrove steps in. 'Girls, you really need to get out and start shooting. We have very limited time to gather our footage, remember.'

'But . . .' says Lia.

'It's not fair,' says Tia.

'Go,' says Mr Trench, and the Flirt Twins pick up their equipment and bicker their way out of the door.

Gemma reluctantly shifts towards me and Drew.

'It actually might be an idea if you *did* stay with George, Gemma,' Ms Cosgrove says, carefully avoiding Mr Trench's stern eyes. 'It makes sense to keep you working in pairs, so that you each get a chance to try everything. And if Drew is bringing Lex up to date on what she missed yesterday, perhaps Gemma can do the same for George.'

Gemma beams, Drew grins, George looks completely dazed, and I sigh.

'If you're sure that's a good idea, Ms Cosgrove,' Mr Trench says tightly.

'Of course it is. George and Gemma can work on some interior shots, and I'll introduce them to the editing software.' She waves her arms, flapping her flowery batwing shirt and looking like she might take flight. 'Now, then. Time is of the essence and we should get started! Obviously we don't have a lot to edit yet, but you could take a look at some of yesterday's . . .'

I miss the rest because Drew is making floaty, Ms Cosgrove-style gestures behind her back. He looks right at me as he does it. I think he's trying to make me laugh.

I laugh – I can't help it. Plus he has really nice arms.

He picks up our assigned camera bag and mouths, *Let's go*, even though Ms Cosgrove is still talking and flapping.

George gives me a bit of a look as I sneak out with

Drew – something between *Ha, get us!* and *Help, what have we done!*

I'm actually having a really good time. Drew and I wander around, straying off the main path and winding through about a million trees. We pass some ramshackle wooden huts, half hidden in the forest, which Drew says were probably built by the original inmates of the base we're using now. He obviously knows a bit about what goes on at a Young Offenders camp. It's weird to see the man-made structures lurking in amongst the trees – they make the forest seem wild and tame at the same time, plus they're kind of intriguing.

I stop to examine one of them, and Drew leans against a tree, slinging the camera-bag strap around his body as he waits for me. Drew is also wild and tame and kind of intriguing.

I leave the hut and walk up to him. 'Where are we going now?'

He shrugs. 'Don't ask me. I'm totally lost already.'

'How can you be lost?' I tease. 'Base Camp Har Har is that way.' I point to where we've just come from.

'I love the way you call it that.'

'It's what Mr Trench called it. Anyway, we might have walked miles away from everyone else on the course' – and I'm strangely happy about that; it feels secluded here, private – 'but I know exactly where we are.'

'I'm glad you do.' Drew looks serious. 'I haven't got a clue.'

'You'd better stick with me, then.' Uh-oh. That might have sounded a tiny bit flirty.

He catches my eye and grins. Definitely flirty. 'No problem.'

I remind myself he's only like this with me because of the game. I move away so as not to encourage him, and turn my back to inspect another hut. But while I'm doing that, he disappears. I mean it. He totally disappears. When I look round, he is *nowhere*.

If he fancies me, this is a really strange way of showing it.

I walk to a clearing and spin slowly around, surveying three hundred and sixty degrees of forest without Drew in it.

And he has the camera bag!

'Drew?' I try. 'Where are you?'

How am I going to find him now?

Then I see it. An absolutely amazing tree in the distance. It's like one of those storybook trees with massively overhanging bits that touch the ground in a circle and form their own cave. The lower branches are twitching – just the slightest shake, but it's not like the wind-induced swaying of the upper leaves. It's a sign that they've been disturbed.

Drew's in there. I know it. It's just his sort of place

– all unruly and individual, like him. I walk over.

I push the branches aside and edge into the space. It's enclosed and semi-dark; it feels like a different world. The ground is carpeted with masses of colourful October leaves and there are gnarly wooden stumps dotted around. Sitting against the main trunk is Drew, smiling lazily at me.

'You found me,' he says.

I flop down next to him, shifting the camera bag to make space. 'Were you trying to lose me?'

He just replies, 'I knew you'd find me. Isn't this place amazing?'

I nod, breathing in deeply and starting to relax. Autumn leaves, mellow wood, and Drew, so close. I want to bottle this scent and spray it on my skin every day.

'It's an adventure tree,' I say, which makes Drew smile.

He moves towards me a bit, pulling himself up on those strong-looking arms of his. He opens his mouth like he's about to say something, then hesitates and shifts away again. There it is again – what's all this sudden shyness about? Isn't the game supposed to make him bolder around me, the way all those girls have been around George? Shouldn't he be trying to throw himself at me?

Instead, he just looks nervous.

I make a face to break the mood, and he laughs.

I try asking him stuff about school and we start chatting about what he thinks of living down here. He is brilliant to talk to. He really listens as well, and I'm almost tempted to tell him all sorts of details about my life – like about that illness I had when I was eleven, and my troubles at school, and how I thought I was on my way to having a great stepdad until Mum and Martin fell out . . . but it's all way too heavy for the atmosphere in here.

I stick to joking around, bouncing off his words with mine and doing impressions of Mr Trench which make him laugh even more. He gives me his take on Ms Cosgrove in return, scrunching his face into mock sincerity. Drew doesn't do geography, but Cosmic Cosgrove is one of the Year Twelve form teachers so he knows her. And clearly, from what he's saying, he's heard her nickname and knows her favourite words too. Actually, I probably told him about that myself, during one of our chats on the Chairs of Doom. Drew underlines his Cosmic Cosgrove impression with some old song that ends with the words, *'She's cosmic!'*

It's my turn to laugh.

He looks a bit smug. 'She has a daughter, you know,' he says. 'A teenager.'

'Urgh, really?' I can never believe teachers have lives outside school. It's just weird. 'How do you know?'

'Sometimes you're not outside Mr Trench's office to entertain me,' he jokes. 'I have to eavesdrop instead. I overheard Ms Cosgrove talking about her daughter and how proud she is of her. Apparently she's *cosmically* clever.'

'She's probably doing Cosmic Studies,' I say.

'At the University of the Cosmos,' he shoots back, dead-pan.

'Afterwards, she can get a job in Cosmetics.'

'And drink Cosmopolitans,' he adds. 'Listening to Florence and the Machine's *Cosmic Love*.'

'At Cos . . . ta Coffee. I give up. You win.'

Drew grins. 'Nah, you definitely win.'

We start comparing notes about other teachers and he has me in stitches with the stuff he says about some of them. It's weird to look at our school from the point of view of someone who's pretty new there. The rest of us are so familiar with it that we almost don't see it any more. It's like the way the pupils treat each other. We all know everyone so well that we barely even look at each other now – we've had our classmates all worked out for so long. It's fascinating to get Drew's take on things.

After a while he looks at his watch and says, 'Oops. The film course.'

'Oh yeah,' I say. 'That.' I hadn't forgotten, but it's so dark and cosy under this tree, in another dimension.

One with only me and Drew in it. Nice. And why did I just think *that*?

'OK, Lex,' he announces seriously. 'So what do you know about what we're supposed to be doing? I mean, is there anything I need to explain?'

I'm not sure how much Drew has heard about me – I can't really imagine Jess talking to him about anything. I guess he knows I'm an Improver, though, from all our time waiting for Mr Trench together. And yet he has this way of asking questions without making me feel remotely stupid. I don't know how he does it – I'm sure anyone else would have got my back up with a question like that. It could so easily have sounded patronizing, even though I wasn't here yesterday and I have a good reason for missing things for once.

'Um, yeah. Pretty much everything,' I admit, which is rare, for me. I usually lie and pick things up as I go along instead. 'I totally drifted off.'

He laughs. 'Don't blame you. So, OK, you know this film showcase thing at the Bijou on Friday?'

I nod. I try to stop looking at his muscles and concentrate on what he's saying. I absent-mindedly pull my new-look long hair.

'Well, each of our pairs is supposed to make a really short film in a different genre, and then the clips will get edited together and shown with captions – you know, like, *Thriller: Kathryn and Jess, Western: Hayden and Cam.*'

Oh, so that explains the chase through the forest in Jess's storyboard.

'Lia and Tia are filming a nature documentary – Cosmic Cosgrove's favourite.' Drew smiles. 'You and George were assigned "drama" yesterday, but from what I heard, he's doing that with Gemma now, indoors.'

'A hospital drama,' I comment. 'Gemma would love that, and George could so act the wounded person. So what do *we* have to do?'

Drew fixes his eyes on the tree trunk. 'Ah. Yeah. Well, it was Gemma's idea, yesterday. I didn't get a say. I think she thought she'd still be paired with Matt – it was before we found out he wasn't coming back. Um . . .'

Uh-oh. 'What?'

He hesitates for ages. Then he says, 'Romance.'

'No way!' Trust Gemma! And, oh no! *'Romance? That's not a type of film.'*

Drew shrugs. 'I don't know. Romantic comedy, I suppose . . . Maybe we can change it.'

'We're going to have to.' What was Gemma thinking? She's really gone loopy over Matt. It's probably just as well George has saved her with the game. 'I mean, how are we supposed to do *romance*?' I finish.

I realize I've walked right into it now. If Drew wants to make a move or anything, following the game settings, then I've totally given him a chance by saying that.

I sort of wait for him to scoop me in his arms and say something cheesy like, 'This is how we do it, Lex. You and me, sitting in a tree, K-I-S-S-I-N-G.' Only slightly more romantic than that, obviously.

I'm thinking I wouldn't mind.

But instead he does the shy thing again and says, 'I don't know. I suppose we could just film a romantic atmosphere or something, couldn't we? Ms Cosgrove would like that.'

'Yeah, and now you sound like her!' I laugh. 'What's a "romantic atmosphere"?'

'You know . . .'

'No, I don't.'

Drew frowns. 'Come on, Lex. You do know . . .' He looks around. 'Like right now, for example. Don't you think? It's all kind of dark and private here and . . .' He gives up. 'Leafy.'

I laugh. 'Leafy? Ooh, how romantic! Leaves!' I stand up and start kicking a pile of them around, going, 'Oh wondrous leaves! I luurve you, leaves! Leaves totally put me in the mood for romance!'

He laughs and pulls the camera out of the bag. 'See? Perfect. I'm filming it. You can be the beautiful romantic heroine, skipping through the leaves because she's in love.'

I kick leaves at his jeans as he stands up. 'Aren't we supposed to storyboard and stuff first?'

'You could do it afterwards.'

'I'm sure that's not how it works.'

He looks at my backpack. 'Storyboard it, then – quick!'

'Aren't you going to help me?'

'No.' He reaches back into the camera bag, pulling out pieces of equipment. 'It's not my thing.'

'Hey! Aren't we *both* supposed to do *everything*? Isn't that what Ms Cosgrove said?'

'Who cares what we're supposed to do?' Drew's such a rebel. 'You can assign me something, if you want – a thing you don't help me with. If it makes you feel better.'

'I feel fine.' More or less. I watch as he plugs the small boom microphone into the back of the camera. 'But you can be in charge of sound, then, if you want.'

He nods. 'Deal.'

'You're not the kind of guy who follows the rules, are you?'

He does his trademark eyebrow-waggle. 'You'd be surprised.' He fiddles with the mic, clipping it into the holder.

'I bet I wouldn't!' I walk right up to him. 'Jess has told me all about you.'

'Jess doesn't know everything about me.' He points the camera at me and pretends to film from close range. 'And she's barely told me a thing about you. I wish she would.'

'Why do you wish that?'

He lowers the camera and looks cornered. 'Because you're . . . I don't know. Interesting.'

'Interesting?' Ugh. 'That sounds so *boring*!'

Drew laughs. 'Well, you're definitely not boring.'

He lets the camera drop gently to the ground next to us. It was the only thing between us, and now we are close. Really close. We stare at each other, and I think we're both breathing strangely. Well, I know I am, seeing as I'm actually thinking about breathing, and normally it's something that just happens . . . like breathing.

I'm thinking about everything, in fact. I'm thinking about Drew's expressive eyebrows and I'm definitely thinking about Drew's lips. And his gaze on *my* lips . . . and how easy it would be to lean forward now and just . . . kiss him.

So it seems that Drew is right about leaves being romantic after all. Huh.

Or maybe everything's romantic with Drew around. Even the Chairs of Doom.

Argh, what am I *thinking*? I am back with Matt! I've been waiting for this chance for months!

This is so definitely George's fault for changing Drew's *Love* settings. Though if he's trying to make a point about how attracted to Drew I am, then he might be kind of succeeding.

Drew says, 'So . . . we'd better start filming.' But he stays where he is.

'But don't you . . . don't you want to kiss me?' I say. Well, actually, I *know* he does, because of the game. But people are not supposed to know things like that about other people, let alone mention them. The second the words are out of my mouth, I want to put them back.

'Lex . . .'

'Actually, forget it,' I say as casually as you can say anything, after you've asked someone if they want to kiss you. And they, you know, haven't.

Drew steps back, turning away from me. 'Talk about mixed signals,' I think he says.

I get a horrible embarrassed rush of heat to my stomach. 'What did you say? What do you mean?'

He turns back but doesn't look at me. 'Nothing. Nothing – sorry. Let's get to work.'

I really hate it when I ask people what they've just said or what they mean and they reply 'Nothing'. It drives me absolutely crazy. Even if Drew doesn't know me all that well, I'm really shocked that he's just done that to me. I thought he was on my side! I thought he understood me! We've been chatting for ages! We're Improvers together! I (almost) saved him from the broken Chair of Doom!

My head pounds. I reach forward and grip his shoulders, forcing him to look me in the eye and see exactly what I think of him. I try to fill my face with murderous intent, but then it mixes with a fleeting thought about how nice it feels to touch his upper arms. Which is ridiculous, because I'm really, *really* angry with him right now. And there is absolutely *no* reason to do what I do next – which is to fling myself at him and kiss him. Passionately. On the lips.

But I do it anyway. He stumbles back in surprise, but I move with him and keep kissing, and within seconds he's kissing me back. We mesh together, and when his arms tighten around me, mine encircle him instinctively and my kisses turn deep and hungry. I've never kissed anyone like this. Drew is amazing. His kisses are blowing my mind.

I break off to take a gulp of air. 'You're really annoying,' I tell him. My anger has somehow disappeared, though, and I'm sure I don't sound like I mean it. I also ruin it by kissing him again immediately afterwards. I can't help it.

This time, he breaks away first. He pauses, but he's still out of breath when he says, 'See, *that's* what I meant by mixed signals.'

'Oh. Right.' I do sort of see what he means. 'Sorry. I didn't mean to . . . pounce.'

Drew locks his eyes on mine. 'Um, Lex,' he says, taking my hand and swinging it in his. 'It's OK. I didn't exactly . . . mind.' His eyebrows do their thing at me. 'In case you didn't notice.'

'Oh. Good.' I think.

'And sorry if I upset you with what I said. It's just that I really wanted to . . .' His expression goes all shy again. 'But I got a bit . . . scared and confused. And then I felt stupid. Sorry.'

'Oh.' *Scared?* When he could easily win Olympic Gold for his kissing abilities? Confused I can relate to. 'It's all right.'

His mouth melts into a beaming smile. 'Good.'

Yes. Good.

Good? No – bad! Help, what have I done? Because, I realize, I started it. I can't exactly blame the game, or George, for the way I just snogged the face off Drew.

But I'm pretty sure he only went along with it because of the *Kiss* setting.

We're still holding hands. This is all wrong.

He kicks at the ground. 'So . . . I get that you don't want to see *Lord of the Rings*, but if you ever *did* want to go out sometime, somewhere else . . .'

Oh, no. The *Date* setting! Him asking me out is *definitely* because of the game. There is no way a boy like Drew would ask a girl like me out otherwise. Anyway, this wasn't supposed to happen. This wasn't in my get-back-with-Matt plan. This *is* George's fault!

I let go of his hand. 'I can't,' I say.

'Oh.' The smile leaves his eyes. 'OK.'

'Yeah.'

'Yeah.' He stirs a mound of leaves with his foot. His

legs are all muscle. 'Is it because . . . you're grounded, or something?'

Ah, here's my Improver status kicking in. He automatically assumes I'm in trouble. But I can't really complain about that when I've spent the last two months inventing stupid and terrible crimes to make him laugh outside Mr Trench's office.

'Because if you are, maybe we could . . . I don't know . . .'

Also, I might possibly *be* grounded after this morning. But still. 'No, it's because . . .' The reason feels all sketchy in my head, like it's been half erased. 'It's because I'm going out with someone else,' I admit. I wait for the swell of pride I felt earlier about finally getting back with Matt.

I don't feel it.

Drew's eyes have grown dark. 'Right. OK. I didn't know.' He actually seems . . . hurt.

Oh help, what am I doing? Now I just want to kiss him again. And my brain is totally going: *Matt who?* In fact, it's going: *'WHO who?'* because I can barely even remember the name of . . . That other guy. Not when Drew's eyes are on me.

'Sorry,' I mumble.

He looks away. 'Yeah . . . Let's get to work on that film.'

'Um . . . yeah.'

145

Then I do think about Matt. Have I actually just cheated on him with Drew? When we've only been back together for one morning?

But Matt and I didn't kiss, so maybe we're not *officially* together yet, and anyway, what just happened with Drew is never going to happen again. Ever.

Drew and I talk politely to each other as we sort things out, focusing on the task and avoiding any kind of physical contact. If Mr Trench could see us now, two of his Improvers working mega-hard on the course he's forced them to go on, he'd be totally proud of himself for his wicked punishment skills.

'Well, that was the weirdest day of my life,' George says later, when we're up in his room eating Martin-made biscuits again. I've come straight here from the course today and I know Mum won't like it, but I figure I'm in so much trouble with her already that a bit more grief won't matter. Besides, I plan to be asleep by the time she's home from work, and awake too late for her tomorrow. Hopefully by the time she finds time to speak to me, she'll have forgotten what her issues were (though she'll probably have replaced them with all-new ones).

'It can't have been weirder than mine,' I say. I haven't told George what happened in the Adventure Tree, and I don't think he could have guessed, because Drew turned out to be amazingly diligent for a notorious Non-Attender. He insisted on getting back on time, with everything all sorted, and we worked pretty well together, if I say so myself. He did the sound and I worked on the storyboards and we both did everything else, with an absolute minimum of contact between us.

Maybe if our classmates were acting halfway normal they'd have suspected something from the way Drew and I were carefully polite to each other for the rest of the day. But they were all acting just as crazy as they had in the morning, with the exception of Jess, who did her usual Jess thing of hanging onto Trenchie's every word, and Kathryn, who was more about the shy glances at George and less about full-on fawning in the style of Lia, Tia and Gemma.

'So what happened to you today?' asks George, but he doesn't wait for an answer before he adds, 'Wow, Lex, all those *girls*! They really seemed to like me.'

'Oh yeah,' I remember. 'I meant to tell you – I have a great idea about the Jess thing. If you change Jess's *Life* setting to make her more laid-back, then she might stop focusing on work so much and notice *you* instead. Don't you think?'

'Um, yeah,' George says, which is weird on two counts. One: because George doesn't say 'yeah' if he can say 'yes' or even 'affirmative, Captain'. Two: because George doesn't look particularly interested.

'Jess? Girl who stole your heart in Reception?' I remind him. 'You've chased after her your whole life? It's Jess you want, isn't it?'

'Yeah. Yeah. Definitely.' He doesn't look very definite. At all. 'It's just . . . can't we keep today's settings for a bit longer? We haven't really given it a chance yet, have we?' He shifts uncomfortably. 'I think Jess should have another day or two of seeing how popular I am.'

'OK, George.' I sit forward on his bed and lean towards his computer chair, cupping my head in my hands so I can see him clearly. 'Tell me what's really going on.'

He wriggles like a demented jellyfish. 'It's just . . . I think that if Mr Trench and Ms Cosgrove hadn't kept hanging around us today, Gemma would have . . . kissed me.' Squirm, squirm. 'She definitely wanted to.'

Oh God! Of course, because of the settings. I'm not really sure why this makes me feel so weird – it's not like the Matt thing at all. But it just seems so . . .

'It's wrong, I know.' George nods. 'I wouldn't have let her, not when I know it was all because of the game.'

I think for a second. 'Hold on, George! Is that the *only* reason you wouldn't let Gemma kiss you?'

He frowns. 'What do you mean?'

'I mean, maybe you wouldn't let her because she's Gemma. And you don't fancy her.' *And she's utterly evil to me*, I don't add. He wouldn't see that the way I do. I still expect his loyalty, though.

148

I wait for him to confirm it.

He doesn't.

My heart starts hammering, even though I tell myself this is stupid. I'm the one with the Gemma issues, not George. She's really pretty. He *might* fancy her, I suppose. Ugh! But it's none of my business.

I ask him outright. 'Do you fancy Gemma, George?'

He hesitates, and I feel like throwing a pillow at him. 'You're going to kill me if I say yes, aren't you?'

I throw a pillow at him, and it misses and lands on Gollum the Laptop.

'Hey!' He pats Gollum lovingly. 'I didn't say yes!'

'You might as well have done!'

'But I *don't* fancy her, not exactly! It's just that ... Gemma's really good-looking. Girls like her don't normally look twice at me. Well, girls of any kind don't normally look once at me. Now suddenly I have three of them all over me, and—'

'Four.'

George frowns.

'Four. Gemma, the Flirt Twins and Kathryn.'

'Oh, I don't think Kathryn was interested after all,' George says. 'Maybe the game didn't work with her. Do you think it's because we didn't fill in her profile properly?'

'No, Kathryn was definitely into you,' I inform him. 'Believe me. I saw her. She just wasn't as obvious as the others. Different sort of person. But seriously, George, what about Jess? One day of attention from girls like Gemma and you've forgotten the girl of your dreams?'

Honestly – *boys*! Jess is so right about them.

'I haven't! I swear. But I'm sort of . . .'

I give him a stern look.

'I'm *enjoying* it, Lex.' He sighs. 'Come on, tell me you didn't enjoy Drew being after you? I saw the way he looked at you all afternoon, like he wanted to eat you whole.'

I get a hot flash of embarrassment. 'Even if he did – which he didn't – how could you have seen that when you were so busy fielding girls, George?'

'I only had to look over for two seconds. It was clear.' He sits up. 'Look. This is the weirdest thing in the world. But we're just using it to help us, aren't we? I was thinking today that we should set out some guidelines. Establish some rules of play.'

I groan. 'Oh, I am not discussing any more of those long-winded role-play games with you.'

George sets his face to 'long-suffering'. 'I'm not talking about *World of Warcraft*, Lex. Not this time. All I mean is that I agree with you. This game is fun, but it's completely wrong if we take advantage of anyone as a result of our settings.'

I gulp. 'You agree with me? Wait, did I say that?'

'You didn't have to. You told me you didn't actually

kiss Matt this morning, and I think you were absolutely right not to.'

I decide not to tell him that it was only because my mother was there and/or I had morning breath.

'So that's the main rule,' he says. 'No letting anyone kiss you when they're under the influence of the game. Makes sense, right?'

'Um . . .' Oops. I think about Drew in the leaves and my cheeks burn.

'Secondly—'

'There's more?'

'Secondly, no more changes to the *Looks* settings. It's too hard to explain away.'

I pull at my top and narrow my eyes. 'You'd better not be thinking about what I think you're thinking about again, George.'

He looks indignant. 'I was thinking about my eye colour, actually. Kathryn came up and asked me about it today – she asked if I wore coloured lenses sometimes.'

'Ooh, she noticed! *Told* you she likes you! Are you going to snog her?'

'No, Lex,' George says patiently. 'Remember what I said two seconds ago? Anyway, even though we should stick to those rules, we can still use the game to help us. For the future.'

I do a *Huh*? face at him.

'You know how the game expires on Friday? Well, I

asked Dad about it this morning. He says all the settings get frozen when a trial game becomes inactive.'

'Frozen?'

'Yes. Set for ever as they are. Then that's it. Game over. You just uninstall it.'

'You mean on Friday, the wind changes and we all stay like that?'

'That's right. Thursday night is our last chance to change anything.'

'So if we leave the settings as they are, you could have Gemma and the Flirt Twins after you for ever?' And I could have Drew.

Um, I mean Matt.

'Yes. Except that would be wrong.'

'Yes. Wrong.' Aw.

'So we need to set everything back to normal on Thursday night. You know – clean slate, like before we started altering things. It's the right thing to do, isn't it?' George looks as doubtful as I feel. 'I mean, you can't really force people to go out with you, can you?'

'Or kiss you,' I say, trying desperately not to think about Drew in the Adventure Tree.

'Yes, I know you agree with me. They have to really want to, or else it's not right. But if we use it just to, you know, *help* us. So that they've noticed us, and maybe they look at us differently after the game's over but

152

they're using their own free will . . . Then I think it's OK, don't you?'

'So we use the game to give us an advantage, but after Thursday we're on our own?'

'Exactly. I know people are already seeing me differently. Maybe if we make enough of an impression, their feelings will linger, and things could work out for us. Lots of girls will still fancy me, which means I have a chance with Jess, and you have . . .' He gives me a look.

'Matt,' I say after far too long a pause. I immediately distract George with, 'So you're still after Jess, then? Because that's not what it's been sounding like.'

He sighs. 'Lex, I think I might be after *every* girl.' He gives an apologetic shrug. 'I'm not proud of myself.'

'You can't have *all* of them. It's selfish. Besides, I couldn't stand it if the Flirt Twins fell out, you know, over *you*. It's disturbing the natural order.'

The corners of George's mouth twitch upwards. 'OK, I'll give up Lia and Tia,' he concedes, and I try not to notice that he's not giving up Gemma.

He opens the game on Gollum and I move over to sit beside him. I link Lia to Hayden and Tia to Cam, a combination that has happened in the past but lasted about one end-of-party apiece. George points out that this is a good thing because if they happen to snog, then it's not messing with nature – it's only re-igniting what has gone before. I ask if this means I'm allowed to kiss Matt despite Rule One and George says, 'It doesn't count for you because you know about it.'

I'm officially *never* telling him about what happened today between me and Drew.

We leave the rest of the settings the way they were.

The next morning I have ten messages from Matt, making increasingly desperate-sounding arrangements for our date, which has to be Thursday night now because of some 'family thing' he says has come up. He sounds so keen and excited about going out with me that I totally forget about Drew. I have to replay the Adventure Tree scene in my head in graphic detail about twenty times first – just so I can let it go, that's all, because I've already been thinking about it all night. Apart from that – Drew who? I am Team Matt all the way.

I roll my eyes when another message comes in from Matt and I write him a quick reply to shut him up.

Thank God, L! Thought you'd gone off me, he texts.

I don't know why George isn't already tired of this game-induced desperation. I remind myself it's only for a couple of days, by which time Matt will genuinely want to go out with me and we'll be all sorted, according to George's plan.

So what's up? I text, in reply to yet another message saying he wishes he could see me sooner.

Family stuff, Matt writes back, followed by: What time can I see you?

The family stuff can't be too terrible, then. I think about what Mr Trench said and wonder whether Matt was just looking for an excuse to ditch the course. It doesn't sound like him – he's not the dropping-out type, not like Drew. I make up my mind to ask him about it tomorrow; after all, we're a proper couple now and we should talk about things like that. Even if we never did before.

I arrange to meet him at our old date haunt. Then I go round to meet my hobbling hobbit, girl-crazy friend next door so that we can head off for another fun-filled day at the film course.

When we reach the hut, I'm not exactly surprised to find that Drew's not there. I'm disappointed when we're sent off to work in our pairs, though, and there's still no sign of him.

'Alexa, are you OK on your own for now?' Mr Trench asks me. He seems to be relaxing quite a bit and booming far less, three days into the course. Ms Cosgrove hangs back, smiling and at one with the cosmos. In fact, everything in the hut is a hundred per cent calmer today. Lia's smiling at Hayden and Tia's flirting with Cam and they're totally getting on with each other. It's like harmony has been restored to all my friends. Even Gemma, fussing over George's bad foot, looks much happier, obviously not seeing Kathryn's shy smiles at George as any kind of threat, and Jess is once again in hard-work heaven and oblivious to all the secondary school trysts going on around her. George really should have changed her *Life* setting – I don't know why he never listens to me.

Mr Trench seems to reconsider. 'If you prefer, you can stay here with George and Gemma and help with the editing.'

'Um, no,' I mumble in horror. 'I'm fine by myself.'

'Good for you. I'm proud of your spirit, Lex. It's essential that we keep going, despite absences,' he says.

Omigod! Mr Trench called me 'Lex'!

He lifts his chin to address the room. 'OK, good luck, guys!'

He said 'guys'! Our teacher is turning into some kind of seriously chilled-out dude.

'Remember that tomorrow is mainly for editing, and Friday morning we pull everything together as a team before the final showing at the Bijou. Make the most of your final day of shooting!'

I trudge off to the Adventure Tree by myself and try to pick up where we left off with the slightly weird 'romantic' short. The story goes: girl kicks leaves happily, girl falls in leaves, girl clutches heart in lovesick pain and covers herself in leaves. Then we repeat the same scenes with just a boy. We called it *The Stages of Love*, and the pain was completely Drew's idea. He wouldn't even look at me when he suggested it.

We were going to shoot the stages in order according to my storyboarding, but Drew kept mixing up the scenes and I decided we should go with his take on things. After all, love is a big mixture of that stuff, really, in any order. It's also deeply confusing. Like, for example, if I love Matt, why can't I stop thinking about Drew?

I change the focus for a long shot of a pile of leaves, but it's hopeless without Drew – I mean, there's just no action, for a start. Besides, I miss him. So I put the camera down and lie back on the crunchy ground. Maybe I even doze off for a bit because the next thing I know, Drew's there. Lying next to me, looking super-hot.

I jump and sit up.

He sits up too. 'Hi,' he says.

'You gave me a heart attack!'

'Sorry. I tried to get your attention but I think you were daydreaming.'

'Oh. How long have you been there?'

'About two seconds. I had a bit of trouble finding our tree.' He frowns. 'I can't seem to navigate very well without you.'

'Well, you should have come here *with* me. Why were you so late?'

He goes a bit shifty. 'Oh, you know . . . I struggle with mornings.'

'Yeah, I know. Wild parties.'

'There you go again. Is that really what you think of me?' he asks, though he says it lightly.

'It's what I *know* about you. You're a total bad boy.' I grin.

He laughs and his eyes sparkle. 'You don't know me at all.'

'Oh, you'd be surprised.' Oh no, I think I might be flirting with him again. What would George say?

But I can't help myself. Drew is so gorgeous, and he's in a way better mood than he was after what happened yesterday. In fact, I think he might be flirting right back. And anyway, it's not as if I'm going to . . . God, I really want to kiss him again. I bite my lip. I promised George. Last time I kissed Drew, we didn't have rules yet so I wasn't *really* breaking them. Now we have rules.

'Go on, then. Tell me all about myself. Surprise me,' Drew says, pulling a jacket out of his backpack and handing it to me. 'Pillow,' he explains before he lies back down on the ground with his head resting on his deflated bag. I settle my head on his jacket, which smells gorgeously of him. It's really pretty intimate, lying side by side in the shade of the Adventure Tree like this. I take a couple of deep, jacket-scented breaths before I say, 'OK. I know you're one of Trenchie's Improvers.'

'Improvers?'

'Yes, you know. Mr Trench never tells people off properly. He just says we should focus on *improving* things, one step at a time. That makes you and me Improvers.'

Drew smiles. 'Oh, you mean because of our lunch-time visits? I've actually started to look forward to those.'

Ooh. So have I, if Drew is there, but I don't tell him that. Instead I continue. 'I also know that you're an Improver of the Second Kind. A Non-Attender.' I realize that he's never actually told me this, but it's obvious: I rarely see him at school unless it's outside Mr Trench's office.

He laughs. 'Of the Second Kind? How many kinds are there?'

I prop myself up a bit so I can list them on my fingers. 'There are people like you who spend their days at the arcade . . .'

He laughs again.

I ignore him and tap another finger. 'There are the ones who keep getting into trouble – that's Type One. Then there are the completely brainless ones. Those are Improvers of the Third Kind.'

His brow creases. 'Um, shouldn't you say the ones

who aren't achieving academically, or something? It's just that people can't always help learning at different rates, you know. "Brainless" is a bit harsh.' He seems slightly embarrassed, but sure of himself. 'I'm just saying.'

He looks right at me like he's trying to read me, or something, and now I *really, really, really* want to kiss him, as opposed to before, when I just *really, really* wanted to kiss him.

I wish George and I had never touched that stupid game. This isn't supposed to be happening, and I can't even act on it.

Maybe I should ask George to change the settings back a day early, even if it means Drew won't want to know me any more. It's better than feeling like this – like he actually might be interested in me and I desperately want him to be.

And like I want to kiss him but I really shouldn't.

'Lex . . . ?' he says. 'You OK?'

In fact, maybe I should just put Drew right off, right now, instead of waiting for the game settings to do it for me.

Maybe I should just tell him the truth.

So I say, 'Actually, Drew, I *did* mean brainless, and I'm not being rude because I'm one of them. In fact, I'm the only one.'

His expressive eyebrows go up. 'But you're one of the trouble-makers. You've told me yourself.'

'Yeah, I do get into trouble for stuff sometimes,' I admit. 'But mostly I have to see Mr Trench a lot because I'm the school's only Improver of the Third Kind.'

He looks completely shocked. 'What?'

Oh, wasn't that clear? 'I'm the only person in the school who's properly thick,' I explain.

'Lex!' Drew leans towards me, his eyes flaring. I try not to notice the heat of his body, so close to mine. 'That is ridiculous. If that's what Mr Trench has been saying, then we should report him!'

Eek. 'Trenchie doesn't say that,' I tell him quickly. 'He's always telling me I'm capable of anything, and all that stuff he's been taught to say.' I laugh, though it's not remotely funny. 'I'm the one who nicknamed us Improvers and split us into categories. I made it up when I was bored on the Chairs of Doom.' Before Drew came along. 'And I *am* thick, Drew, I swear.' I do an all-body shrug. 'Don't worry, though, it's no problem. It's just one of those things.'

Drew frowns but doesn't say anything more.

Then he reaches over and touches my hair, and I don't even mind – not like I used to if Matt ever did that. I know my hair is magically longer now, but the way I've lost my self-consciousness feels like more than magic.

Oh, he is gorgeous.

Also, I don't seem to have put him off me by

admitting that I'm thick. Why did I think I would? He's a rebel – he's not like perfect Matt.

Or maybe he's not put off because he's set to like me. Maybe nothing I say will affect him. Not until we alter the game settings.

Drew's expression is intense. 'You can swear all you like, but I know you're bright and funny and wonderful.' He gives a little laugh. 'Apart from the fact that, right now, you're talking rubbish.'

I echo his words from before. 'You don't know me at all.'

'So . . . change that,' he says softly. His eyes are full of questions.

I don't let him ask. Instead, I find his lips with mine and the air around us crackles.

We kiss and kiss, and it's even better than yesterday. My head fills with Drew and my body cranes towards him and I can't help it. I can't! Our kisses get deeper and hotter, and we are seriously in danger of setting the romantic leaves on fire here.

He breaks away, breathless, and I have to stop myself from grabbing him and pulling him back.

Between short gasps he says, 'You're going out with someone else.'

'Oh.' My heart's pounding like mad. 'Yeah.' I stare at his lips. I want to glue them to mine. I want to kiss, not talk. 'Yeah, I am.'

'Yeah.' His smile doesn't reach his eyes. 'And I'm not sure if you've noticed, but you're kind of doing the mixed-signal thing again, Lex.' He clears his throat. 'In a way. You know what I mean?'

'Oh,' I say. 'Yeah.'

Would it make things worse if I kissed him again?

Probably.

I could try, though . . . Like, as an apology.

I move forward.

Drew moves back.

'Sorry,' I say.

'It's OK.' He gives me a long look that makes me shiver. It also makes me want to kiss him, but I've recently concluded that pretty much anything Drew does has that effect.

'So . . . is this person you're seeing . . . is it serious?'

Oh. Yeah. Him.

Well, I want it to be. At least, I *think* I want it to be. I've wanted it for ages. I can't have changed my mind that easily. Can I? And anyway, Drew was my distraction, the person I tried to fancy to stop myself thinking about Matt. I wasn't supposed to succeed quite this . . . successfully.

'I think so,' I answer.

Drew's face clouds over. 'OK, so . . .' He turns away completely.

'So?'

163

I'm not sure what he says next, but I watch him pick up the camera and concentrate on changing the settings to film in the half-light of our tree.

My legs aren't the only part of my body that don't work properly when I scramble to my feet.

My brain, for example, seems to have totally forgotten why I wanted to get back with Matt.

Thursday starts off way more peacefully than it ends.

I don't go to George's on Wednesday night – I'm kind of scared of talking to him because of not wanting to admit the Drew thing – but he doesn't seem to want to chat anyway. When Martin drops us off, he barely says goodbye to me before he disappears into his house. Admittedly, he has been looking exhausted. Maybe all the female attention is wearing him out.

I put it out of my mind and focus on avoiding Mum for the second night running. This involves watching out of the window for her, spotting her and then diving into bed and pretending to be asleep for approximately half an hour, after which it's safe to assume that she's engrossed in the telly and I can get back on the computer without having her turn up in my room for the serious chat she's been wanting.

I manage the pretend-sleep thing again in the morning when she pops into my room before work. This is much easier to achieve – I know exactly what time she has to leave. My only problem is that my phone keeps vibrating with incoming messages on my bedside table. I sense Mum walking over, and there's a moment when I think she's going to read my messages, which will make it impossible for me not to sit up and shout at her. But she hesitates, strokes my hair lovingly and totally respects my privacy.

The only downside of *this* is that I then feel guilty for having avoided her since Tuesday. I just can't win with Mum.

When I'm sure she's gone, I pick up my phone. The messages are all from Matt, and all looking forward to tonight.

This is it. I'm going out with Matt again. Woo. Etc.

The day at the course goes OK, though it's a bit different because we're all together as a group, looking over footage and making suggestions for each other's films. When it's time for *The Stages of Love*, a Lex and Drew Production, I keep sneaking little glances at Drew. He is so definitely avoiding my eyes.

He actually arrived on time today but Jess didn't make it at all, which is extremely weird. At least it gives me an excuse for something to talk to Drew about at lunch time, because suddenly I feel like I need it. Well, I *need* an excuse and I *want* to talk to him.

By the time I've eaten my lunch on a bench outside and plucked up the courage, though, I can't find him. I walk past Cam and Tia and Hayden and Lia, pairings which seem to be working out pretty well. I go back into the hut, where George is in a corner talking to Kathryn for a change, and Gemma is nearby shooting daggers at them. No Drew anywhere. Maybe he's being told off by Mr Trench . . .

I have a quick peer into the side room, but Drew isn't there. And my peer isn't nearly quick enough because Mr Trench appears at the door.

'Lex!' he says, using his new name for me.

I mean, it's nice of him, but it's also a bit unnerving. I resist the temptation to reply, 'Trenchie!'

'How are you enjoying the course, Lex?'

I mumble something and hope it sounds positive.

'Good, good. I wanted to tell you that I'm extremely impressed with the quality of your work. You obviously have a gift for film-making and an eye for the shot. And I'm very pleased with the way you and Drew have been working together. The two of you really gel, don't you think?'

Um . . . yeah. That's one way of putting it. I nod and concentrate hard on not blushing. I'm so glad the Adventure Tree is in the most secluded part of the forest and there's no way anyone has witnessed the kissing.

'I've seen the storyboards too,' Mr Trench adds. 'Impressive. And did Drew actively help with those?'

'Kind of,' I mumble. I refuse to land Drew in trouble.

How does Trenchie even know to ask about that? It's like he has a sixth sense – the ability to sniff out the tiniest amount of rebellion.

'I see.' His nod doesn't give away what he's thinking. 'Did you do *everything* together?'

Yeah, I wish. And now I've definitely gone bright red.

'Drew did the sound on his own,' I admit. I don't mind getting myself into trouble – I can take it. I wait for the booming to commence.

But Trenchie actually smiles. 'Well, great. It's about teamwork, after all. I'm going to be awarding you and Drew a special certificate after this course, Lex. I'm seriously impressed with your progress.'

Ah, I get it. He's motivating the Improvers.

'You should know that the certificate is worth its weight in gold,' he continues.

'Is it made of paper? The certificate?'

Mr Trench gives me a strange look. 'Yes.'

'It's not very heavy, then, is it?' I remark. 'Not much gold. Not enough to get rich or anything.'

'No, Lex,' Mr Trench says patiently. I can't seem to wind him up any more – I've lost my touch. 'But it's a huge accolade. And if nothing untoward happens between now and the end of the week, then I'd really like you to help out with the continuation of the course at school after half term. What do you think?'

'Um . . . continuation?'

'Yes. An after-school club, probably one day a week. We can make sure we open it up to *all* students, not just the mainly Gifted and Talented who signed up this time.' He smiles like he and I are in on a joke. 'And the people whose parents or guardians I spoke to. People who were initially here against their will.'

Ah, *that's* the joke. He's talking about me and Drew and our elaborate detention.

He doesn't look like he's joking, though, when he adds, 'People who have, quite frankly, exceeded the standard of the Gifted and Talented and should be very proud of themselves. So will you consider it?'

Uh-oh. 'Wouldn't it be better for someone like Jess? Or Matt?' I ask him, temporarily forgetting that perfect Matt shamed himself on the first day and never came back.

'I'd really like *you* there, Lex,' Mr Trench insists. 'I think you could be a real inspiration to our other students.'

'Oh.' Oh, *inspiration*? I'm not sure I like the sound of that, either.

'I'd like to ask Drew too. You're absolutely shining examples of what can be done . . .'

What can be done if you're hopeless Improvers and you actually turn up for a change, and locate the brain cell required to press RECORD on a camera?

I let Mr Trench go on with his praise, and when he

ends – with 'So what do you think?' – I say, 'Yeah, sure, fine.' But I know I won't do it.

The worst thing is that Mr Trench has taken up the remaining lunch-break time I was going to use to find Drew and . . . whatever I was going to do when I found Drew. I'm very annoyed with my heart for racing at *that* thought, when I didn't even think anything racy. My heart should just watch out, really, for the times when I really *do* give it something to race about. At this rate, it will probably explode.

I cool myself down by texting Jess: Where R U?

She replies: Home! and I'm about to ask her whether she's OK when Mr Trench and Ms Cosgrove troop in for the start of the afternoon session.

Drew slinks back in much later, as we finish going over the footage. It all seems to take ages, and afterwards Ms Cosgrove looks at the clock and has a sudden meltdown, complete with arm-flapping.

'Students! We've run out of time to prepare for to-morrow!' she announces, going blotchy red with panic. It's like she's switched places with Trenchie. Instead of all her usual cosmic love, she starts having a go at us for being absent (Matt, most spectacularly, but also Jess today), persistently late (Drew), constantly distracted (Gemma, Lia, Tia, Cam, Hayden . . . that list is long), and even injured (George). I notice George slipping guiltily down his chair when she does that, and Kathryn shooting murderous looks at Ms Cosgrove. These are followed and easily matched by the daggers Gemma aims at Kathryn.

Mr Trench steps in with a calming hand on Ms Cosgrove's shoulder. Total role reversal. She gives him a look that makes me wonder for one icky moment whether there's something going on between those two. Shudder. I shake the terrible thought out of my head. The game is driving me a bit crazy – I've started to think everyone's connected by secret *Love* settings.

Mr Trench tells us all we still have a couple of hours tomorrow morning to get *something* ready for the big show, even if it isn't exactly as finished as we'd hoped. He says we'll manage it, and anyway, we're all in this together, and we're all together, together, together. I wait for him to burst into a song from *High School Musical*. Right now, I wouldn't put it past him.

When the day finally ends, Drew runs out before I can attempt to get him on his own (listen, heart, that is *enough!*), and George is behaving even more strangely than yesterday. He doesn't talk to me at all on the way home, and tries to rush into his house as fast as his one and a half legs can carry him. I grab hold of one of his crutches as he passes by and he's forced to stop.

'Hey, let go,' he says. He frowns at me. 'Lex, you should never come between a man and his mobility.'

'I don't see any men around here,' I comment, because

Martin is already in the house. He's left the door open, probably thinking nothing of the fact that I've stopped George out here. After all, it's not like we don't normally talk all the time.

Except these last couple of days.

'So what's going on?' I ask. It's more of a demand, though, really.

George shifts his weight. It is a hop of guilt. 'What do you mean?'

I only have to give him my knowing look for about ten seconds before he's blurting it all out.

'I'm so ashamed of myself, Lex!' he confesses. 'You heard Ms Cosgrove today. I think I've ruined the final film by getting injured!' He looks miserable. 'It's all my fault our film won't be ready in time.'

'Come on, it was an accident,' I reassure him. 'Besides, Ms Cosgrove didn't say it was *just* your fault. She blamed lots of other people—'

'Like Matt?' he says accusingly. 'Didn't he leave the course as a direct result of us changing his *Life* settings? Because whatever was going on in his life, he wouldn't normally have sounded off like that in front of Mr Trench.'

'Well . . . there is that.'

'And all the others who are barely concentrating because they only have *love* on their minds? Because of the game?'

'Most of them normally behave like that anyway.' I smile, but he still doesn't. 'And they haven't *all* been that bad.' I think about Drew, who has worked pretty hard, really. Despite a few moments when his mind was on . . . other things. Like kissing me. I try not to lose myself in that thought.

George says, 'And all *I* can think about half the time is how I don't want the game effects to wear off. Ever. I am enjoying it way too much. It's worrying.'

'Is that what you were thinking about all the way home yesterday? When you wouldn't talk to me?'

'Maybe. Yes. It's not that I *wouldn't* talk to you, it's just that . . . I know you don't really approve of certain settings.'

Before I can stress too much about the girls who are currently in love with him – namely Gemma – he puts my mind at rest.

'Plus I was thinking that I wanted one more attempt at getting Jess to like me before the game's over,' he adds.

I nearly jump up and down. 'So did you do what I suggested? Did you change Jess's *Life* settings last night to make her more laid-back?'

He nods. 'Only she was so relaxed that she didn't even turn up today . . .'

I think about the text at lunch time. 'Oh yeah. She was at home.'

'I thought it must be something like that.' George's brow creases. 'And her absence only made things worse for the course. So there you go. It's all my fault, Lex!'

OK, that's enough. 'Look, if it makes you feel better . . . surely it's half *my* fault? I was involved in most of the game settings too.'

'But it's *my* game.' George is behaving like a three-year-old.

I put my hand on his arm, which makes him totter a bit, adding to the toddler effect. 'Come on, it's not *that* bad. It'll be OK.'

He steadies himself and shakes his head. 'It won't. Not unless I can think of a plan to sort things out. Like . . . I don't know. Going back to the hut to get the film ready right now . . . or at least bring us up to date.'

'Right *now*? George, are you crazy? Base Camp Har Har will be locked! You know what the teachers are like about all their *precious* equipment.' I do a little Gollum impression when I say the word 'precious', but it barely brings a smile to George's lips. This proves how seriously distressed he is right now.

'Look, why don't I come in,' I suggest. 'We can eat your dad's biscuits and figure something out, even if it takes all night.' I can't have George not laughing at my Gollum impression – it's not right.

He looks at me. 'Lex, aren't you forgetting something?'

I don't think so. 'What?'

'Don't you have a date tonight? With Matt?'

Oh. Yes, I have. I've been collecting texts from Matt all day to prove it, and then it nearly went out of my head. How weird.

'And it's the last night of the game,' George says. 'So I have to wipe the settings tonight, don't I?'

'Oh, yeah.'

'So it's your last chance with Matt . . .'

He's right. I have to impress Matt now, while he's under the spell of the game. Then, as from tomorrow, he'll *want* to be with me.

'If that's still what you want,' George adds, looking almost . . . hopeful. Hopeful that I'll say no, that is.

I wave his hope away. 'It's definitely what I want! And you're right – I'd better start getting ready.' I need to do something about the look on George's face, though, or I won't be able to enjoy my getting-back-with-Matt triumph. 'Listen, George, don't worry, OK? About the course, or Jess, or me and Matt, or the game. Any of it. Promise me you won't worry.'

'Hmm,' he says.

That's not good enough, so I go for a cheesy saying instead. 'Remember you're the Lord of the Ring! You have the power.'

'Honestly, Lex! It's not exactly a *good* thing,' he says, but this time he smiles. Then he goes all quiet and super-thoughtful again, so I decide I've probably done as much as I can.

I say goodbye and practically skip away. I am so excited about my date with Matt.

At last!

All I've wanted since summer was to get back with Matt. Matt is perfect! I was so happy when I was going out with him before. What's going on?

We're sitting in silence in the chippy. It has a little restaurant at the back and that's where we always used to meet, so it's kind of our place. I don't think Matt comes here with Gemma. (Or *came* here with Gemma – they've split up! I keep having to remind myself.) Gemma looks older than me, and they can probably get away with going to the Red Lion, which famously serves sixteen-year-olds. But with me, the petite half-elven girl, Matt has to go to places like this.

I think about the fact that, if I'd kept my new, game-inspired figure, I might have got away with the Red Lion too. At least if we'd been in a pub there would have been lots of other people around. Here there's just me and Matt and an elderly couple in the corner, and it's so quiet they can probably hear the grains of salt falling off the chips I'm sharing with Matt.

Well, I say 'sharing' but he isn't even eating.

I have three more chips and then I try: 'Are you OK?'

'Yeah.' Matt gives this huge sigh, which is definitely not a sign of OK-ness.

I half wonder whether George changed his *Life* settings again, because he's almost behaving like he was on Monday with Trenchie. Then I remember that his life isn't so perfect anyway, what with his 'family stuff', or whatever. The way he acted before might even be a display of the way he's really feeling. Maybe he has serious issues behind his golden-boy exterior. Maybe he's tortured and misunderstood by everyone, including me.

'So . . .' I try, giving him a chance to open up to me. 'What's going on at home?'

'At home?' he asks.

'Your family stuff,' I prompt. 'The reason we couldn't go out yesterday.'

I've been friends with Matt for ever and went out with him for five months, but right now he feels like a stranger. How did we used to talk to each other? I really don't remember.

'Oh.' He grimaces. 'Yeah. That. My gran's living with us at the moment and she's a total pain. Mum's trying to get her into a care home but it seems to be taking ages and she keeps having a go at the manager, which maybe doesn't help.'

'Your mum has a go, or your gran does?' I smile.

He doesn't. 'Mum. Though you should hear what

Gran says about them too. Anyway, Mum, Dad and Chloe keep dumping Gran on me when they have to do other stuff. That was what I had to do last night, and Tuesday too. I'm like an unpaid babysitter, or something. She even made me put *Emmerdale* on the plasma screen when the match was on. She's such hard work!'

Matt's making his gran sound like a troublemaker – like some kind of elderly Improver. I feel myself warming to her instantly, taking her side against her moaning grandson.

He whinges a bit more, adding something really rude about the care home manager, the kinds of words I used to think were out of character for Matt until the *Life* settings thing on Monday. It seems like people stay within their own limits even when they're changed by the game, though.

'Is that what your gran said?' I joke. 'I like her style.'

'No, that's what *I* said, Lex.'

I grit my teeth. 'Yes, I know. I was kidding.'

'Oh.' Matt's eyes soften, like he's remembered why he's here. 'So, Lex, I'm so happy we're back together. I've been thinking about you a lot . . . ever since Tuesday morning.' He frowns. 'Weird, huh?'

Um . . .

'So it's good to see you. And can I kiss you now?'

He's robotic. I can't believe I ever told Drew that leaves weren't romantic. The most shrivelled bit of

177

foliage is about a million times more romantic than Matt is being right now. How can he say words like that with so little emotion in his eyes?

I think of George's rule with a weird relief. 'No, it's not a good idea,' I tell him.

'Oh.' He looks put out.

There's a massive silence while neither of us can think of anything to say. Well, I can't think of anything, and Matt doesn't even seem to be trying.

I kind of wish I was with George right now, helping him wipe the settings of the game. I sigh. This is supposed to be my big chance to get Matt. My *last* chance, seeing as the game ends tomorrow. I've been dreaming of this for ages.

I come up with something to ask him. 'What did you think of the film course, then?'

He picks up a chip. 'Rubbish,' he says. He waves the chip around instead of eating it.

'Oh.' He didn't exactly try it for long, though, did he? 'So why'd you sign up for it in the first place?' I select a chip for myself. 'I didn't think you and Gemma were into—' Uh-oh. This seemed like a good thing to talk about, until I blurted out the name 'Gemma'. But on Monday he was still very much with Gemma. Still. Why did I say that? It's like I can't stop thinking of him and Gemma as a couple, no matter how desperate I've been to split them up.

178

A strange expression flits into his eyes. 'Gemma,' he says. Then he puts the chip down as his face goes a bit crumply.

What?

Gemma?

Did my date just pronounce the name of his ex-girlfriend and look like he wanted to cry, despite the fact that I've totally made him want to be with me through the power of some kind of freaky gaming force?

This has got to be the worst date I've ever had in my whole life. Does he miss Gemma? Had he forgotten all about her until I mentioned her? I don't exactly want to, but I feel I have to say, 'What *about* Gemma?'

'Gemma,' he repeats. 'You asked why I did the course. Well, Gemma. She's the reason.'

Now I can't stop myself, even though I don't really want to talk about Gemma, because this is just weird. 'Don't you mean *you're* the reason *she* took the course? You signed up and she followed you?'

'Not really,' Matt says. 'It was more the other way round.'

That doesn't sound right. 'But it had to be your idea,' I insist. 'You always join stuff. You're super-boy, team-player, join-everything-face and everyone loves you.'

Matt gives a little smile – the first I've seen all night. He didn't even smile at me when I arrived, and I spent two hours getting ready. I couldn't have looked

179

much hotter if I'd used magical games to help me.

'I don't think I am,' he says. 'I've been really down lately. Haven't you noticed?'

I shake my head. He's been a loved-up love-puppet to Gemma, as far as I can see. Well, apart from what happened on Monday, but that was different.

'Well, I have. All this stuff with my gran, you know, and then there's my sister . . . It's getting me down! So Gemma made me do the course. She always knows what's best for me. She makes me do stuff to stop me from getting all depressed.'

'That's rubbish.' Isn't it? 'You don't get depressed. Do you?' Maybe he does. I think back. I can only remember Matt laughing away with his mates and being generally well-liked for no particular reason. For being utterly *normal*.

'Yeah, I do. It's, like, last week Chloe borrowed my razor to do her legs and she totally blunted it. I was *gutted.*'

'OK, Matt, but that's "being annoyed with your sister". That's not "depressed".' I manage to stop myself rolling my eyes because he seems so serious about it. And also kind of up himself.

'Gemma thinks I was, and Gemma's mum's a nurse.'

'So is mine,' I remind him, but he ignores me, so I don't add the part about my own opinion of his condition.

Diagnosis: arse.

He mopes. 'Gemma always knew how to cheer me up. Gemma's, like, my rock.'

Gemma, Gemma, Gemma. This is unbearable. 'Maybe you should go out with Gemma instead of me, then,' I say, though I realize how ridiculous this is, seeing as that was the problem in the first place, and I've made this happen.

Matt looks startled. 'Oh, sorry, Lex. No, I definitely want to go out with you.' He frowns, like he doesn't quite understand his own feelings. 'It's just that we were happy, me and Gemma.' He looks confused. 'She felt really bad when you finished with me, you know.'

'She told me that,' I say, resisting a sudden urge to run away. Gemma told me she felt responsible for splitting up me and Matt, right before I stopped talking to her altogether – at least when other people weren't around.

Because Gemma *was* responsible for splitting up me and Matt.

She must have felt about as bad as any evil genius feels when their wicked plan succeeds. Bad in a maniacally laughing, white-cat-stroking way.

'Gemma really cares about people,' Matt says.

This sparks my anger at both Gemma *and* Matt. Has he forgotten what happened?

'You know, Matt,' I say, trying to keep my voice level, 'it was Gemma's fault you and I broke up.'

He doesn't say anything. He just looks at his chips.

OK, this actually *is* the date from hell. A recording of this date is probably used in the training course for hell-hounds on how to make hell more . . . hellish.

'Gemma made up lies about things you said,' I continue, feeling the odd need to explain his own life to him. 'She did it on purpose to break us up. And she broke us up so that she could get together with you.'

There. I can't say it more clearly than that.

Matt doesn't make any move to speak.

'And, listen, I'm sorry I believed her and didn't give you a chance to explain,' I add. I've been wanting to say these words for months too, but it's weird how little relief I'm feeling now I've finally said them. 'I just got angry, you know. But we're back together and every-thing's OK now, isn't it?' Even *I* can tell how hollow my words sound right now.

He's finding the chips fascinating.

'Matt, did you hear me? I'm sorry I believed Gemma. I'm glad you're not with her any more. She's evil.'

Matt perks up. 'Gemma's not evil. Gemma's amazing. And I can't believe the way you've treated her when she was just being a good friend to you.'

Well. This is *not* in the film I've been directing in my head – the one of me and Matt getting back together for ever. I stare at him.

'The way *I've* treated *her*?' I say.

'I mean, the way you pick fights with her over stupid stuff at school. Gemma has told me about it, Lex. Maybe our other friends haven't noticed, but I know. It's really hurtful for her, and really childish. And I know you're not perfect but I never had you down as being so immature, you know?'

I find myself gripping the table, speechless.

Not perfect? Immature?

Matt reaches for my hand. 'Don't worry, I still want to go out with you. I just want you to know that the way you've been with Gemma is out of order. She was only trying to do the right thing.'

I move my hand as far from his as I can. 'Did you hear me?' I pronounce carefully. 'I said Gemma made up *lies* about *things you said* so that she could break us up.'

Matt shakes his head. 'Gemma doesn't lie.' He frowns in confusion. 'Lex, I've been thinking about you since Tuesday morning. Can I kiss you?'

Oh God, that is so annoying. I ignore it and take a deep breath.

'Matt, if Gemma doesn't lie, then what she told me is true. Is that right?'

His mouth stays closed. I feel my voice start to shake.

'So, hold on, let me get this straight. Did you really tell your friends that you were only going out with me because *you felt sorry for me*?'

'My friends are your friends, Lex,' Matt says. 'Hayden

183

and Cam, mostly. No one important. And I wasn't really going out with you, was I?'

We've veered way off script now. This is a whole different film.

'Matt, I went out with you for five whole months, until Gemma . . .' She didn't lie to me about what he said. 'And then I dumped you.'

'We were *seeing* each other,' he insists. 'It's not the same.'

OK, I'm not playing this game. 'Going out, seeing each other, snogging at parties and going for chips and sending slushy texts – whatever you want to call it. That's not the point.' I take a deep breath. '*Did* you tell Cam and Hayden that you felt sorry for me?'

I believed Gemma when she first told me what she'd heard. It was only after she got together with Matt that I decided it was part of her evil plan to snaffle him. I'd been going out with Matt for ages, after all. I was not someone Matt *felt sorry* for.

Matt lowers his eyes. 'Look, Lex, you've already given me enough grief. Don't dredge this up again. It's not *my* fault if people took it the wrong way.'

Is there a *right* way to take it? 'What did you mean, then?'

'Just . . . you know. That I didn't want to break up with you because I didn't want to look heartless. I'm not heartless, you know.'

Oh. Oh. 'Because you *feel sorry* for me?'

He shrugs. 'They're just words, Lex.'

I force myself to breathe. 'Just *words*?' Just humiliating words.

Just the words I was scared that everyone was thinking anyway.

Just the words I couldn't even tell my other friends about afterwards because I didn't want to say them out loud. I couldn't even tell George about what happened between me and Matt – and Gemma – in case the 'just words' weren't . . . just words.

In case other people felt the same way.

Even my other friends. Even Cam and Hayden. Even Jess.

Even George.

I didn't want to risk seeing it on their faces.

'Lex, come on.' Matt gives me a pleading look. 'Cam and Hayden laughed it off. It was nothing. If it wasn't for Gemma, you'd never even know I said it.'

I might throw the salt and pepper shakers at him. 'Even if you hadn't said it, it's bad enough that you felt it. Anyway, don't you *mind* that Gemma told me?'

He shrugs. 'I get that she was being a loyal mate. Look, I didn't mean to upset you. I really didn't. I'm sorry about that, even if you never gave me a chance to apologize at the time.'

185

I almost can't look at him. Especially not after what he says next.

'But Gemma's right. You bring it on yourself a bit, Lex. I mean, you should hear yourself right now . . .'

'What? *What?*' So now it's *my* fault Matt said something shamefully insulting to his friends, something I've been hoping for months he didn't really say?

And *Gemma* is right? Gemma, who said I 'bring it on myself'?

'You're always so down on yourself, Lex. So defensive. Gemma told me you didn't even sign up for that film course until Mr Trench forced you to, even though you've always wanted to work in films – be a director or something.'

I can't believe he's been discussing me with Gemma. I feel sick. 'I've never said I want to work in films.' I'm sure of this. I've only ever said it to myself. 'I'd never say anything like that.'

'Yeah, but it's obvious how much you love them. You're always in the Bijou and hanging around with George the film nerd when you think no one's looking. And that's just it.' He sighs. 'You're always worried about what people think of you. Isn't that partly why you went out with me? For your image? I mean, a bit . . .' He smiles.

I pick up the salt shaker. I am *this* close now. 'I thought you'd just decided we weren't actually going out?'

'Come on, Lex . . .'

He is unreal! 'No! You're wrong!'

Though I remember what I told Mum that day. *'He makes me feel normal.'*

And isn't that why I wanted him back?

I wanted the feeling of *normal*.

Matt shrugs in that easy-going, charismatic way of his. 'OK, then. Sorry. Again.'

I nearly say *That's OK*, as a reflex, and then I think of shouting that it's really not OK. But somehow I can't manage to be angry any more. I put the salt shaker down.

My heart is sinking because I think he might be right and the whole thing is just too horrible.

I went out with him for his image and how popular he is, and he didn't break up with me because he felt sorry for me.

And Gemma spotted what was going on, in her usual Gemma ever-analysing way, and stepped in to sort things out. Or rather, trampled over me to take what she wanted.

Matt frowns like something has just snapped in him. 'Never mind what happened before. I'm not with Gemma any more. I can't stop thinking about you, Lex. I want to kiss you. That's what counts, isn't it?'

No. No, it isn't.

It's time to go. I don't say anything to Matt. I just

leave, as quickly as I can, trying to ignore the looks the old couple give me on the way out.

Annoyingly, Matt catches up with me outside almost straight away. He grabs my arm and pulls me towards him. 'Lex, none of this matters. Didn't you get what I said? I really want to be with you now.'

'Don't,' I say, but for some stupid reason I let him hug me and I bury my head in his familiar muscle-bound Matt-type shoulder. I want to cry. Here's Matt, desperate to be with me after George and I have worked magic on him, and he still doesn't think particularly highly of me. The only reason he has his arms around me right now is the game. It's as bad as the Drew thing. No, it's worse. I'm not even sure that I'm all that attracted to Matt. He's right. I was using him before. I was using him to boost my flagging self-esteem, and even that didn't work.

Also, I need to be honest with myself. The truth is, when Gemma told me what Matt had said, I believed it because I could imagine Matt saying it. Because he *did* say it. I've always known he wasn't the person I wished he was – the perfect boy, someone who could magically make me normal and accepted. He was just Matt, a guy at school, kind of hot in an ordinary way. He got together with Gemma, and I brainwashed myself into thinking it was all some horrible mistake and I should never have broken up with him. When really our relationship was all wrong from the start.

'Lex, I can't stop thinking about you. Can I kiss you?'

Can he? Does it matter how wrong we were together before and how right I was to finish with him? He wants me now, and I want this. Don't I?

Matt bends to claim the kiss I made him crave. I'm back with Matt. It's what I've wanted for months.

It isn't real. And even if it was, I wouldn't want it.

I pull away and tell Matt I have to go.

I head straight for George's house.

Martin lets me in and I try to exchange the shortest possible piece of smalltalk with him. He's talking away animatedly but I don't really understand a word he's saying. I'm utterly focused on the need to get to George – now. Or at least to the game. I need to change those settings right this second, or make sure George has already changed them. I do not want Matt to want to kiss me for one second longer than necessary. I wish George and I had never started messing with the game!

Martin excuses himself and heads back to his basement with a bewildered look on his face, like he doesn't quite understand how he landed in his own life.

I run up the stairs and burst into George's room.

It takes me a few seconds to realize that he's not in his usual place, at his desk.

Then I yelp, leap out of the room and slam the door behind me.

Because George definitely wasn't at his computer.

He was on his bed. With a girl.

With a girl!

George was on his bed with a girl!

I only saw a blur and not much else, so I don't know which girl it was, but it was definitely George and a girl!

I lean against the door and breathe, grasping the door handle for support. OK, OK, it's not so weird. George is a boy, and he likes girls, despite what my mother thinks. He likes them so much that he's got loads of them magically obsessed with him. Plus he has a broken toe. If one of the girls came round, it might be more comfortable for George to sit on his bed to talk, and the girl might sit there with him and . . .

Who am I kidding?

George was on his bed with a girl!

And what about the no-kiss rule? What happened to George's principles, and waiting until the effects of the game had worn off?

I can't believe my girl-crazy friend! I can't believe I felt guilty about breaking George's rules by kissing Drew, when George is just as bad! I am having serious words with him . . . as soon as I can breathe again.

Unless the girl wasn't one from the game. What if it was . . . Jess? But surely that isn't possible. Could my idea have actually worked?

The door shakes behind me.

I do not want to think about what is going on in there!

Then I register that the handle is straining under my hand. Oh. George – or the mystery girl – is obviously trying to open the door.

I step aside and the door opens a crack. Then a little more. Then George hobbles out through the gap and shuts the door behind him.

'Lex,' he says, propping himself up against a wall. He adds, 'It's not what you think.'

'I'm trying not to think. Is that Jess in there?'

He shakes his head. 'I've accepted it's never going to happen with me and Jess. You were right, Lex. And maybe . . . maybe I don't want it to any more. I'm starting to realize that now. Jess is a dream. I want a real girl.'

I'm too stunned to say anything. Who *is* this 'real girl', and what has she done to change George's mind about a girl he's worshipped for most of his life?

He looks nervously at the door. 'You know I would have invited you over too if I hadn't known you were out. What happened with Matt? Why are you here?'

'*Invited me too?* Ugh! Stop! And never mind about Matt.' I feel wobbly. The Matt thing, and the way I've been with Drew, and now George. It's all too much.

He looks worried. 'Oh no – are you OK?'

When I don't answer, he says, 'You need to sit down.'

'Well, I'm not sitting on your *bed*!' I lean against the wall instead. 'There's a *real girl* on it!'

George moves so that he's leaning opposite me, still casting glances at the door. 'Honestly, Lex, there was nothing going on . . . I mean it!'

'I don't believe you! Why else would you take her to your *room*? You have other rooms! You have a huge front room downstairs. I've always thought it would make a great party room if you, you know . . . were the party sort.'

George looks hurt. 'So I'm not the party sort?'

'That's not the point. Boys aren't supposed to have girls in their bedrooms!'

'You're in my room all the time!'

'I don't count!' How many times do I have to tell him? 'She counts! Random *real girl*!'

'But she asked to see my *Lord of the Rings* poster.'

I'm on a roll so I don't even dwell on this outrageously bad chat-up tactic. 'My mum goes crazy if I'm in *any* room alone with a boy, let alone a *bed*room!' She used to kick up a right fuss when Matt was round, even if he was just in the kitchen getting a drink or something. She'd suddenly come in every two seconds with urgent questions about daft things like whether my PE kit was clean.

'My dad doesn't seem to mind.' George's eyes cloud over. 'Maybe Mum would have minded. I don't know.'

'Oh.' Oh yeah. That shuts me right up. 'I'm sorry.'

'No, no,' George says quickly. 'Lex, don't worry. It's

OK.' He looks like he means it about as much as if he'd said, *Be my guest – and why don't you rip a few pages out of my favourite books and maybe pour Coke over Gollum the Laptop while you're at it.*

Or maybe that's not what the look on his face is saying. He's definitely displaying some kind of pain, though. 'There's nothing to be sorry for,' he says. 'You can't avoid talking about mums around me, can you? I always talk about my dad, don't I?'

I've never had a dad, though. My mum was a free spirit, wild-child type who got pregnant in her late teens – probably after having a *boy* in her *room*, come to think of it. The closest I've ever come to having a dad was when Mum was with George's dad, though even when that was over it wasn't as if Martin went out of my life.

'It's not the same, is it?' I say.

George shrugs, still with that pained look on his face. He puts a hand on my arm. 'Lex, I'm worried about you. Please will you tell me what happened with Matt?'

'I'll tell you later.' And I think I really might tell him all of it, this time. 'But first – this is more important. I rushed over to check about the game—'

'Oh, I need to talk to you about the game! Just—' He breaks off suddenly.

'What?'

George coughs awkwardly, his pained look deepens, and I freeze.

The bedroom door opens and I remind myself what's going on here. There's a girl in that room – a girl who has caused me to stand and talk to George on his landing – and I don't know who she is. And it shouldn't matter. Now I've calmed down a bit, I can see that. I mean, good for George, right? I know he's never had a girlfriend and I know he really, really wants one, and increasingly he doesn't seem to care who exactly it is. This isn't any of my business. I possibly even encouraged it.

But I'm not sure if any of this applies if the girl is my worst enemy in the whole wide world.

If, for example, the girl is Gemma.

Because that's who appears at the door, all pretty blonde hair and boy-attracting curves.

Gemma.

'Oh. Lex,' she says casually. 'I thought I heard you. And saw you walk in on me and George.' She wiggles her hips at George, totally flirting. *'Together.'*

He goes bright red.

She has arrogance and triumph written all over her. If I didn't know about the game, I'd be sure Gemma was only doing this to upset me.

It certainly doesn't seem like there was nothing going on, anyway, despite George's insistence.

There's an extremely long pause in which no one says anything, and then, irrationally, I feel a surge of anger at

George that is easily as strong as the one I've been feeling towards Matt and Gemma.

I can't believe he's dropped Jess . . . for Gemma!

And what about George's principles and all that stuff about not taking advantage of the game?

I stand up. 'I'm going. I'll leave you two to it. And George . . .'

'Lex?' His eyes fill with misery and guilt. *Guilt* – that's what the pained expression has been all along!

'You've changed,' I tell him.

I turn away. I can't believe I actually felt bad about kissing Drew in the Adventure Tree and breaking George's 'rule'. At least Drew has a soul!

I plan to charge out of the house, slamming the front door in a dramatic exit, but I only get as far as the bottom step when two girls stumble into the hallway, clutching drinks and looking around.

'Hey, it's Lex,' says Lia, one of the girls. 'Have you seen Hayden?'

'Lex!' says Tia, the other one. 'Have you seen Cam?'

I give them a long look and then step into George's airy front room – the one that would be perfect for a party. Lia and Tia follow me, dancing into the room towards a heavily loaded tray of drinks. Kathryn is there too, shyly bopping about on a patterned rug. And Jess is dancing on a coffee table around a pile of TV guides.

It seems that George is having a proper party

featuring the entire female contingent from our film course. Except me.

Even though I noticed straight away that Jess is in George's front room dancing on a table, it takes me a bit longer to register the following:

Jess. Is in George's front room. Dancing. On a table.

This is turning into a night of surprises.

'Jess!' I call to her. 'What the—?' I get the impression she can't hear me anyway, so I let rip. I finish with: '. . . are you doing up there?'

She looks down and then jumps off the table, landing in a jazz-finish with her arms outstretched and her fingers waggling. I recognize the move from something she used to practise with Matt's sister Chloe at lunch times, back before she decided she was too serious for dancing.

She does a perfect little bow and then shouts something at me, but I can't make it out so I drag her into the kitchen, where hopefully she can talk normally.

'Lex! I'm so glad you're here,' she says as soon as we get there.

'Jess, I'm so . . . shocked you're here,' I say. 'What's going on? How come George is having a party on a Thursday night?' Or any night, really. And more to the point, 'How come you're here? And why weren't you at the course today?'

I know the real answer, of course. George changed her *Life* settings, and this slightly scary version of Jess is obviously the result.

'Didn't feel like it!' Jess says, and she starts dancing on the spot. 'Needed a break! GCSEs are months away!'

I can't believe what she's saying. Last week she was stressing about exams starting 'in only seven months' time'. Just the mention of the word 'GCSE' normally has her breaking out in a cold sweat and locking herself up in a fort of books.

Now she sings, 'I want to DANCE!' She does a couple of carefully executed Lady Gaga moves. No one's going to reach *her* on the telephone tonight. 'Who cares about school stuff!'

It's like she's being as dedicated about dancing and not-caring as she normally is about schoolwork.

I kind of want to reassure myself that she's still Jess, even though I know what's happened. '*You* do. *You* care.'

'I *normally* care,' she laughs. 'But right now, I'm lost in music!' She morphs into an elaborate Michael Jackson medley, complete with moonwalk and tipping of an invisible hat. It's the exact routine she did in her dance-class show last summer, the term before she gave up dancing for ever. I remember I went to see it with Matt's whole perfect family (minus the rebel gran) because Chloe was in it too. Gemma insisted on coming with us

– to see Jess, she said. But she managed to sit next to Matt. It wasn't long before Matt and I broke up.

'Jess, what happened to you today?' I ask.

'I wanted to know what it felt like to bunk off school. I told Mum I was sick and then I legged it to the park!' She laughs. 'It was a bit boring there, though. I spent a bit of time sitting on the swings sending silly text messages to annoying people, and then I went home.'

'But it's a holiday course! You weren't even *told* to go on it by Mr Trench. That's not proper skiving.'

'I know,' she says sadly. 'I need to do better.'

OK, so she *is* still Jess.

She wiggles her hips. 'Next week I'll try skipping school instead.'

'Jess!'

My dorkily perfect friend focuses carefully on being carefree. She jumps up onto the kitchen table and launches into a macarena, which plays havoc with Martin's mug tree. Naff choreography – definitely Jess's idea of rebellion.

'Jess, please get down,' I say, feeling about a hundred years older than her.

She won't listen to me, so I leave her throwing all her dedication into sashaying around a teapot, and go and find George. Never mind how angry I am with him for snogging Gemma – I want to make sure he's changed every single setting back to normal. *Now*.

* * *

I can't see George anywhere obvious so I creep up to his room again. This time I knock and wait for about a minute before I carefully open the door. I edge my way in, but there's no one there. Who knows where George has got to, or with which girl? I'm not sure I even *want* to know.

I look around the familiar room with all the *Lord of the Rings* posters and *Harry Potter* collectibles, and I sigh. This game has changed my friend. I want him back.

I sit at George's desk and open up Gollum the Laptop. The screen instantly lights up with *Pygmalions* and goes straight to Jess's profile. It shows that her *Life* settings were adjusted at 11.59 last night, which makes me think George was hesitating about changing it. Anyway, I put it right. According to the computer, there are just over two hours left of tonight, and I can't believe George hasn't already set everything back to normal the way he said he would. Just when I thought I couldn't be any more annoyed with him!

I'm so totally focused on changing settings – even my lovely hair: it has to be done – that it's a shock when someone taps me on the shoulder, right after I adjust the last setting. I spin round in George's chair.

It's Gemma.

'Hey, Lex,' she says. 'Playing with George's toys?' She sits on the bed opposite me, back where she was when I burst in before. Her bum's perched on an enlarged picture of Ron Weasley on George's *Harry Potter* duvet cover, but she still manages to look cool and glamorous. And evil.

I resist the temptation to bring up Gemma's profile right now and do something nasty to her *Looks* settings – something which, in just a couple of hours' time, will stay like that for ever.

'You're the one who asked to see his *Lord of the Rings* poster,' I say coldly.

She laughs. 'You can't stand the fact that I was up here with George, can you?'

'I don't care at all,' I lie. 'And since when have you been after George anyway?' I feel like getting at her in any way I can. 'You always used to call him a nerd.' And Matt told people he felt sorry for me. We were the most useless bunch of mates in the world – no wonder our group's been falling apart.

A confused shadow crosses Gemma's arrogant expression. 'Since Tuesday morning,' she says, reminding me of Matt now, 'I've been wanting to kiss him.' She bites a nail and frowns.

'What about Matt?'

She kind of shakes herself, completely losing her earlier attitude. 'I love Matt,' she says uncertainly. 'I honestly didn't mean to get together with him in June, but . . . he sort of needed me and I was there . . . and it happened. Look, I'm sorry, Lex.' She turns automatic again. 'I want to kiss George.'

I'm not sure I can go through any of this again.

'Gemma, listen to yourself. You're not making any sense.'

Gemma's face falls. 'You really hate me, don't you, Lex?'

I don't know how to reply to that.

I thought I did. After I spoke to Matt I was even more certain. Even two minutes ago I was fairly sure.

Faced with her right this second, all confused and vulnerable and . . . well . . . under the spell of the game, I'm not so sure.

What I'm really thinking is how much I miss Gemma. Gemma and Jess and I first bonded over a Father's Day craft lesson at primary. None of us had anything like a dad at the time, so the teachers let us make cards for each other instead. Me and Jess and Gemma called ourselves the No Dad Club, and we spent all morning cutting and sticking and making each other happy. Except when Jess and I had a fight about colouring the middle of a flower blue (Jess was horrified; I was determined), and Gemma was the one who got us talking again. Gemma was always like a sticking plaster in our gang, even after it grew to include the boys. Even after she got her string of terrible stepdads, and Jess's mum married Drew's uncle, we were still the No Dad Club together. Until this year. It all started going wrong the day I kissed Matt.

'If you don't totally hate me, can we be mates again?' she says now, and through all the make-up I can totally see my childhood friend. 'I can't stand the way things have been lately.'

'I can't stand it either,' I mutter.

She springs up suddenly. 'I need to find George! I'm so in love with him.'

Oh no – how slowly will the hours before midnight go by?

'Gemma, honestly, you're not in love with George. You just think you are. If anything . . .' And I think I can say it now. Sometimes you just have to face the truth – things move on, they change, and you have to change with them. And maybe it's for the best. Well, this definitely is. 'If anything, you're in love with Matt. And he loves you back, Gemma. You two are—' I resist the strong temptation to say 'as bad as each other'. 'You two are made for each other.'

I realize it's true.

I realize I don't care.

I realize that in some tiny way, Gemma's still my friend and I want her to be happy. Matt's basically a total idiot – how *dare* he go out with me out of pity – but he seems to get slightly less that way around Gemma, at least.

Gemma's face goes all earnest. 'No, really, it's George I love. He's kind and fun. And he's *well* fit—'

I interrupt because that truly is enough. 'And he's also dishonest and selfish. He's been tricking you into thinking these things, and tricking other people too.' I bite my lip. 'And, um, I've been doing it too.'

'I don't know what you're talking about but I know how I *feel*, Lex.' Her eyes flame at me. 'I also know what you're playing at! And you're not going to get in first with the guy of my dreams – not this time.'

'Gemma! You're making it sound like we were fighting over Matt. That's so – ugh!'

'It's so true,' she says with a long blink. 'I don't know what you were trying to prove, but you really hurt me back in January, Lex. You knew how much I liked Matt.'

'But everyone liked him.'

'Not as much as I did, and you knew it. But that didn't stop you snogging him at his party. Well, it's my turn now. You're not stealing another guy from me. George is going to be *mine*!'

'Are you listening to me? It's not *real*. In a couple of hours your feelings for George will disappear. I've changed your settings.'

'What are you talking about?'

I take a deep breath and turn to the computer. 'This.'

Gemma takes a few reluctant steps closer and looks over my shoulder. I show her the game as quickly as I can, before I regret it. I show her the profiles and the settings, and I explain what's been happening. I sense her just shaking her head the whole time. I turn back to face her.

'You've gone mad, Lex.'

'George set you to want to kiss him. He did it on Monday.'

'I've wanted to kiss George since Tuesday.'

'Exactly,' I say. 'The new setting kicked in at midnight. Also, it was Jess that George really wanted, not you. He just thought it would help to have other girls after him, and he had these principles about not kissing people under the influence of the game.' I look at her. 'Which he obviously forgot with you.'

Gemma sort of shrugs. 'Nothing happened between me and George.' She shoots me such a fierce glare that I believe her. 'Yet. He was being all gentlemanly – or possibly scared.'

'Oh,' I say. That sounds like the George I know.

'And I can't believe the lengths you're going to here to get in first with George – inventing crazy stories,' Gemma adds. 'You're getting weirder every day, Lex. You just love the drama of us going after the same boy, don't you?'

'No, I don't,' I insist. 'I think *you* do. I keep telling you I'm not after George, and you keep saying I am.'

She narrows her eyes. 'Yeah, well, maybe I *want* you to be. Maybe I want to show you how it feels when someone else goes for a boy you really like. And don't try to persuade me that you liked Matt too, because I know that to you he was just one of the millions of guys who have a thing for you. Like Cam and Hayden and George and Drew. Everyone always thinks you're so *special*, Lex!'

I manage not to wince at that because it's obvious that she wants me to, and also because I'm thinking, *Wait a minute*. 'Drew?'

Gemma giggles nastily. 'Yeah. He's gorgeous, isn't he? And such a nice guy. And so obviously in love with you. It drives me mad the way you do this, Lex.'

'Do what?'

'You know! Oh, actually, you probably don't, because you're so busy being Little Miss Low Self-Esteem – *Woe is me, I've been ill once and I'll mope about it for the rest of my life.*'

I can't believe Gemma! I can't believe I thought I missed her and could maybe, *maybe* be friends with her again! I was more on the right track when I thought she was evil.

'But it *changed* the rest of my life!' I'm so angry with her for making me say that. 'And I'm not like that!'

'You can be, sometimes.'

'You don't understand!'

'No, I don't. I don't understand how you always get all the guys. George fancies you—'

'He does not.'

'He does. And Drew's in love with you. Matt was with you for months. Even Cam and Hayden pretended to go out with *you* before they pretended to go out with me in Year Eight. Guys always go for you first. You used to be my friend, Lex, but lately your whole super-innocent man-magnet thing has been *worse* than a pain.'

I've had enough of Gemma. I might have got things slightly wrong, and maybe she didn't lie to me about Matt, but I was right all along that she's not my friend any more.

I can't exactly ask her to leave George's room, even though I want to, so I just get up and walk out and I don't look back.

I should go home – I'm in enough trouble with Mum as it is and she's not going to let me avoid her for a third night in a row, especially since I'm too late now to do the duvet-over-head, fast-asleep trick. She's probably already back from her shift and she might even be look-ing out of the window for me. It probably wouldn't be so bad if I arrived home with Matt like I thought I would, but if she sees me walking on my own from the direction of George's house she'll have a proper moan. I wonder if she'd believe me if I told her George was having a party . . .

She'd probably believe that George's dad hadn't

really noticed it and just carried on working, at least, because it's a completely Martin thing to do. I think I'll stress that angle and deflect some of Mum's annoyance, even if I wish she'd stop having a go at Martin.

I'm thinking about all this so I'm distracted as I open George's front door – and walk right into Drew.

I step back, tingling from the unexpected closeness. 'Omigod, who invited *you*?' I blurt, because as far as I could see this was George's total girl-fest. Though Cam and Hayden were probably there somewhere, judging by Lia and Tia's questions.

He gives me a dark look. 'George, of course. Through a text message to Jess. But I couldn't make it.'

'But you're here now,' I point out. I seem to have a sudden need to talk rubbish.

'Yes. Anyway . . .' He cranes his neck to look past me and into the house. 'Is she here? Jess? Can I come in?'

'Oh. Yes.' He's here for *Jess*?

I move aside and he steps in, closing the door behind us.

We both look around. The doors to all the downstairs rooms are open and everywhere looks deserted, even the former party room and the kitchen. Where is everyone?

'So where is she?' Drew asks.

'She was cheesy-dancing on the kitchen counter earlier but I don't know where she is now.'

Drew frowns. 'That's why I'm here, even though I was supposed to be somewhere else. Jess has been acting strangely. I got some crazy texts from her this morning, saying she was in the park. She didn't sound right, so I went to look for her at lunch time. I wanted to check she was OK.'

Ah. That's where he disappeared to. 'Did you find her?'

'No, it's impossible to get anywhere on foot from the forest. I just walked miles, and then I got another text saying she was back home. I made myself late for the afternoon on the course.'

Oh, yes. So he did.

'Then this evening she started talking about us being invited to George's, and Aunt Sarah suggested I should borrow the car to drive Jess over, so I asked Jess but . . .' He hesitates. 'Normally Jess would just roll her eyes and ignore me, but tonight she laughed at me, called me her wicked step-cousin and walked out of the door. No, she *danced* out of the door. Her mum said we should leave her in peace for a while, but when Jess didn't reply to Aunt Sarah's texts, she got really worried about her.' He thinks. 'Actually, so did I.'

'She was probably too busy dancing to reply,' I tell him. I marvel a bit at Jess being so rude to Drew, though she always has been, really. I've never thought about how it must feel to be Drew, on the receiving end. 'But I think she's OK apart from that.' I put a reassuring hand on his arm.

'I hope so.'

He looks at my hand and then at me. Our eyes lock.

I take my hand away. 'Yeah. So you should go. If you have . . . you know. Somewhere to be.'

'Yeah.'

He doesn't move. He keeps looking at me. *Really* looking at me, as if we were in the Adventure Tree instead of by George's front door.

I'm doing the breathing thing again too. We both are.

Why does this always happen to me around him? I've got to stop it. Maybe he still wants to kiss me because of the game, but he won't feel like that for much longer. It will all be over soon.

Drew tears his eyes away. ''Scuse me a sec, Lex.' He takes out his phone, which is a really unusual-looking thing with an extra-large screen and loads of buttons. He looks at it anxiously, pressing a few buttons and reading a message or two.

He starts texting and it seems to take ages, so I take out my own phone and set the alarm to go off at midnight. I want to know exactly when the game's over. I also calculate that I now have less than two hours of Drew fancying me before his blinkers are lifted. I feel like Cinderella, only with zero chance of any glass slippers fitting me in the future.

That's when I realize that this is probably what George is up to with his sudden party. Right now, he still has the power, as I told him when I was trying to cheer him up earlier. He's making the most of his last night of game settings. Including having Gemma in love with him. Ugh.

Just as I think that, Gemma comes down the stairs. I'd almost forgotten that I left her in George's room, minutes ago. I wonder what she's been doing there until now.

She pushes past me and opens the door, barely acknowledging Drew but kind of raising her eyebrows at us on her way out. She catches me looking at her and mouths, *Bye, Lex*, with a massive evil smirk. What is she looking so smug about? Now I'm starting to wonder why I was *ever* her friend. At least she didn't actually snog George. I was wrong to get so upset with him earlier, especially considering what I've been doing with Drew in the Adventure Tree.

Oops, I've started thinking about kissing Drew and he's right in front of me, and I'm absolutely staring at his lips.

Drew looks up from his phone. 'OK, now I'm officially worried about Jess.'

I try not to gulp too obviously. 'She's fine, Drew,' I say. 'Committing crimes against furniture polish in some other part of the house, no doubt – but other than that, don't worry. I'll stay and keep an eye on her if you like.' Oh no, why am I promising that? I was dying to leave this mad party, even now that Gemma has gone. 'You know, because you have to be . . .' Joy-riding, or fighting, or whatever it is Drew gets up to most nights.

'At work,' Drew finishes for me.

Oh. 'At work?' OK, I can adjust to that. I imagine him behind the bar at a trendy but slightly seedy club. Or possibly on the door. He's built enough to be a bouncer, and with easily enough bad-boy attitude.

Oops, I'm daydreaming again – and staring at his arms this time.

Drew fiddles with his phone. 'Maybe I won't go in, though.'

Oh, here we go, Mr Non-Attender. 'No, don't get into trouble with your boss over this. Honestly. I've got it covered.'

'I think my boss would understand, considering she's worried about Jess too.'

The leathery-skinned, chain-smoking club owner in my imagination disappears with a *pop!* 'Your *boss* is worried about Jess?'

'Yes. My boss is Aunt Sarah – Jess's mother.'

'Jess's *mum* employs you?' Wait until my mother hears this! Sarah Hartford, perfection herself, with a teenaged Improver on her staff.

'Yes, at one of her rest homes. I . . . I miss my nan a lot,

211

and Aunt Sarah needed extra night-time and weekend cover, and it just seemed right.'

A gorgeous, caring and kind Improver. He's not half as parent-unfriendly as I've been thinking. Oddly, even though I've had enough of golden-boy types like Matt, Drew's sudden shiny halo doesn't put me off him at all. I can't take my eyes off him right now, for example.

'Plus Aunt Sarah took me in, so . . . Yeah, I owe her. I help the other staff with the first part of the night shift whenever she needs me to, which has been a lot lately. That's why she doesn't mind driving me to the course when I oversleep and stuff.' He shrugs and runs a hand through his gorgeous bad-boy hair.

I can't believe I automatically thought the worst of him. In fact, I'm now thinking I'm as bad as people like Matt, judging other students completely by the fact that they have to see Mr Trench on a regular basis.

Drew studies his phone again.

'Yeah, about Jess . . .' he says, looking up. 'Thanks for offering, but I think you're going to need me, anyway, if you want to keep an eye on her.'

'Why?'

'That was from Aunt Sarah. Jess texted her to say she's gone clubbing, and then she turned her phone off. So we'll need the car if we want to find her.'

'What? Jess isn't here? She's gone clubbing?' *On her own?*

He nods. 'Do you have any idea where she'd be? Where do you two normally go?'

I love the way he thinks we're some kind of club regulars – I still get asked for ID to watch a film that's rated 15. (OK, that's just Mike having a laugh at the Bijou, but still. I completely see his point.)

'Um . . . we don't,' I admit. 'I mostly go to George's house or the Bijou, and Jess normally stays at home studying.' I start to panic a bit. 'Where could she be? Do you think she's OK?'

Drew frowns. 'I know a few places, but they just don't seem very . . . Jess.'

That's more like the Drew I imagined. 'We should try. I'll come with you, definitely.' Mum can wait.

Someone comes up behind me.

'Hello,' Drew says over my shoulder.

I turn round. It's Martin, looking more baffled than usual.

'Oh hi, Martin,' I say. 'Um, I was just leaving. Thanks for having me round.'

'Any time, Lex,' Martin says. 'Though do you happen to have any idea where my son's gone with all his other guests? Only, I heard that dancer girl persuading everyone to go out somewhere, and the next thing I knew, the house had gone quiet. I eventually managed to find my phone to call his mobile but it rang in his bedroom, so he must have forgotten it.' He gives a bewildered frown. I don't think Martin has often needed to ring George, seeing as George is mostly either at school, at home or at the Bijou with me. 'It's just that I'd have preferred it if George tidied up after his friends a bit before he went out. Can you tell him that, if you see him? That he might actually be in trouble, for once?' He makes a stern face. 'Got to do the father thing sometimes, haven't I?'

I mumble, 'Um, I suppose so?'

'Thanks, love. Well, goodnight.' He scratches his head a bit and then retreats to his basement.

I'm stunned – and not just at George being a sudden teenage rebel and Martin half threatening to do his version of 'the father thing' for a change. 'They've *all* gone?'

They must have left while I was upstairs with Gemma. No wonder it seemed so empty when Drew arrived.

'Looks like it,' says Drew. 'Should we be less worried now? You know, if she's with people we know?'

I think about it. My mates all acting strangely and under the influence of the game? Jess making them all go out *clubbing*? George not even telling me they were going, and forgetting his phone?

'No, we should be *more* worried. Let's go.'

We try two shed-type places on industrial estates where the air is throbbing with techno beats, and I hang back while Drew chats to the doormen – who seem to know him, confirming my earlier fantasies about him. But it's too early for the clubs to be remotely busy and both places are sure that they haven't seen Jess or any of our friends. Each time we stop, Drew sends a text to Jess to ask where she is, but by the time he's driven into town and parked in the multi-storey, there's still no reply.

I'm glad we're back in a well-lit place so that I can see Drew properly in all his gorgeousness. Even though, obviously, I'm worried about Jess and not just eyeing up Drew. Much.

He switches off the engine. 'We'll have to walk to the Glass House from here, OK?' he says. He reaches for the door handle.

Fine by me, though I'm dying to ask him something first. 'How do you know all these places?' I blurt. 'You've only been living here since the end of summer.'

He lets go of the handle and gives me a huge smile. 'I make sure I party all night, every night.'

'Seriously?' He doesn't look serious.

He laughs. 'No. I'm at work most nights, and when I'm not, I'm studying or sleeping.' He shrugs. 'I know about these places from my mates.'

'Oh, right.'

'So . . . let's find Jess.'

'Yes, Jess,' I echo as we walk away from the car.

I keep thinking about what he said, though. We reach

the High Street, and Drew decides to stop under a street-light to send Jess yet another `Where are you?` text. When he's finished, I say, 'Your mates who know all the clubs . . .'

His eyebrows go up. 'Yeah?'

'Do I know them? Just out of curiosity. Are they from school?' I didn't think Drew had any friends at school. As far as I can see he's a total loner, the rare times he's there. And 'curiosity' is a bit of an understatement for the way I'm feeling right now. I'd be prepared to consider a small amount of torture to find out more about him.

'From college,' he explains. 'I do some special courses there – they have an arrangement with the sixth form. That's why I'm not in school much.' He gives me a side-ways glance. 'But can we still pretend I'm a terrible truant who lives in a rough nightclub? I don't want you to go off me.'

I can't believe he just said that! I also can't help but smile. Oh no, am I that shallow? Not to mention transparent.

'I'm not going off you,' I say, before I remember that I'm not supposed to be encouraging Drew's game-induced feelings for me, and really shouldn't have said that.

He moves a tiny bit closer without looking at me. 'But you're going out with someone else,' he says slowly. 'So maybe I *am* the bad guy you think I am after all . . .' He hesitates. 'Because I'm finding it really hard to stay away from you.'

Oh wow. Oh wow. 'You don't have to stay away from me,' I say. Not for another hour or so, anyway, after which he won't be interested any more.

But Cinderella got to dance with the prince, didn't she?

My heart thuds.

I reach for Drew's hands and lace my fingers through his.

He looks at our entwined hands. 'Stop trying to drive me crazy.' He carefully extracts his fingers. 'I *do* have to stay away from you. You're with someone else. You said it was serious.'

'It's finished with Matt,' I say, though I know I shouldn't. The game, the game! Drew is still under the influence. George was right. This is wrong! I shouldn't be encouraging him. Or pouncing on him, which is closer to what I'm planning here, though with the obvious limitations of being in a public high street.

A smile spreads on Drew's face. 'Not Matt Henderson? From my year?'

'Yes.' I give him a suspicious look. 'What's funny about that?'

He straightens his face. 'Nothing – sorry. I know you used to go out with him but I heard it was over and he

217

was with Gemma. Anyway, I've always thought—' He stops himself. 'Never mind.'

'No, tell me.'

The smile creeps back. 'Um, sorry. But I've always thought he was as self-obsessed and arrogant as the rest of his family. Except his grandmother, whose behaviour is kind of amusing. She's such a character – doesn't let her awful family get away with anything.'

'Oh wow, you've met Matt's gran?'

'Yeah, she's going to be one of our residents soon. When Aunt Sarah finds a space – and gets over the way Matt's mum spoke to us. They came in one weekend when I was there and it all kicked off.'

I remember what Matt told me on our nightmare date. 'Oh, she didn't only insult the manager, then?'

'Nope, and it wasn't just her, either. The whole family are a bunch of—' He gives me a guilty glance and doesn't finish his sentence. 'Um, I don't know Matt all that well, obviously. I just . . . heard some things.'

I haven't heard a thing, but I can imagine.

Drew looks worried. 'I didn't mean to be rude about your boyfriend. I'm sure he's great.'

'Ex-boyfriend,' I correct him. 'It's completely over, I swear. And I think Matt's a . . . Well, you know. Rhymes with Matt.'

Drew laughs. He hesitates before he says, 'So you're not going out with anyone, then?'

218

The air between us goes still.

'No.' I'm not sure if I said that word or just breathed it. 'Even before, I wasn't. Not really. I got it all wrong.'

'And those mixed signals at the forest . . .'

I know I shouldn't say it.

But I do. 'They weren't really all that mixed,' I say.

I lean towards him.

He jumps and reaches for his phone. He presses some buttons and looks at the screen. 'Oh God, Lex! I think Jess needs us!'

Oh no! 'Why? Is that from her mum? What does it say? Where is she?'

'Look! It's from Jess herself.'

He shows me his strange-looking phone. The extra-large screen displays a picture of a cinema auditorium and I recognize it straight away. It's the Bijou.

Why has Jess sent Drew a picture of the Bijou?

Then I notice the message at the top. It says: Stop txting + leave me alone + tell Mum too! Am fine and doing a dance show here!

'A dance show? At the cinema?' Oh, Jess. I hope George is there to stop her, seeing as this is almost definitely his fault. And also a little bit mine.

'We'd better make sure she's OK, don't you think?' Drew says. He holds out his hand to me and I take it. Oh, wow.

Poor Jess. I really hope she's all right. I can't wait to

find her and make sure, even though a tiny part of me wants to have a go at her for taking over my final hour with her not-so-bad-boy-but-so-so-hot cousin.

Mike is on cloud nine.

'Lex! Hello!' he says, rushing towards me when I walk into the Bijou, still holding Drew's hand. 'We've had record takings tonight! George arrived with this whole group of friends who couldn't get into a club. They arrived in the middle of the showing, but there was no one there so it didn't really matter and I decided to re-start the whole film . . . A few more nights like this and our cinema could be saved!'

Oh no! 'Saved? Is it in danger?'

'Oops. I've been trying to keep that from you and George. I didn't want to scare away my only customers.' Mike shrugs, still smiling. 'But yeah, we can probably afford to stay open for a few more weeks . . . if I win the lottery.' He looks at Drew. 'Oh, hello. I saw you the other day, didn't I?' His eyes drop to Drew's hand in mine. I think Mike has always thought me and George were a couple, even if we never really gave him any reason to think that. Apart from turning up at the cinema together a few nights a week, bickering and squabbling the way we do.

I grip Drew's hand and try to ignore Mike's suspicious expression.

Mike sniffs. 'George is in there,' he says pointedly.

'Mike, it's OK. I'm not going out with George.'

He frowns. 'But why not?'

Why does Mike have to pick *now* to question my relationship with George?

'We're just . . . not.'

'Does George know that?'

'I'm pretty sure he does.'

Mike sighs. 'But you're so right for each other!' He seems to catch himself. 'Er, sorry. None of my business. So you're going out with this guy now?'

Drew holds out his spare hand and says, 'Drew,' but at the same time I mumble, 'Not exactly. It's complicated,' and Drew looks at the ceiling. He also drops my hand.

Mike shakes Drew's hand and gives us a look that says he doesn't really want to know – the youth of today, etc. Then he says, 'Anyway, go on in. Show's only just started – again – and it's a corker tonight. One of the girls George came with is doing a dance accompaniment to the film.'

It has to be Jess. 'She's *dancing* to The Fellowship of the Ring?'

Mike nods. 'Yup. I might hire her, actually. She's pretty good, and it's certainly a bit different. Might be an alternative to finding a signing expert for the times we can't get subtitled versions.'

Mike is really big on inclusivity in his cinema. He's also a bit bonkers, but I don't tell him I think that.

We step into the darkness and I wish I was still holding Drew's hand. Did I really upset him with what I said? But we only have a short while together anyway, and, well, it *is* complicated.

My eyes grow accustomed to the darkness, although there are still some lights on by the stage, and I can't believe what I'm seeing.

Jess is standing on the raised stage bit in front of the screen, doing an interpretive dance to the action. She's quivering and crouching with Gollum, traipsing through forests with Frodo and Sam, swooping with raging orcs.

I scan the audience. The people are scattered, mostly in twos, and I can't really make out exactly who is here, seeing as the couples are glued together.

I bet George is one half of one of the couples, though. So there was really no need for Mike to get so funny with me. I wonder who he's with? Would it even matter if it was Gemma? This is all going to be over soon. In some ways, I can't wait.

In other ways . . . I have to make the most of the remaining time. I grope for Drew's hand in the darkness. He seems to pause for a second but he doesn't pull away. We stand in the aisle holding hands, neither of us making a move to sit down. That would feel like too much of a commitment.

Meanwhile a battle scene makes Jess throw herself about on the stage, clutching her wounded heart in pain. It reminds me a bit of *The Stages of Love* by Lex and Drew, to be honest, only slightly more expressive and interesting. Perhaps we should re-shoot tomorrow morning with Jess as our actress. Though re-shooting now would probably give Ms Cosgrove a heart attack.

Also, Drew will not be interested in me in the morning. *That* thought makes me want to throw myself onto the ground and clutch my own heart. I consider joining Jess on stage.

The scene on-screen becomes tree-filled and menacing, and Jess begins to swish and creep, and I replace that idea with worry about her. Will she be embarrassed about this? Will she ever live it down? Is it all my fault? And George's too – he's the one who changed her *Life* settings. But who suggested it?

Me.

Should I stop Jess?

I can't really ask Drew if he thinks she's OK and whether we should do anything about what we're seeing – not in here. So I grip his hand tighter and pull him back out of the door quickly, before he can object. Mike is standing in the foyer tidying racks of film postcards, so we can't talk there either.

I drag Drew down the side corridor to the secret entrance to the private box. There are two at the Bijou –

it's the beauty of an old cinema – but they're usually closed off and Mike rarely lets me and George go up there. Still, tonight is an emergency and Mike's not looking.

We're halfway up the brightly lit side stairs when Drew stops me. 'Lex . . . where are we going?'

OK. Well, here will do. I sit on the step, forgetting to let go of Drew's hand first and accidentally pulling him down on top of me.

I expect him to make some joke about it, but he just shifts away and positions himself on the step next to me, facing me. 'What's going on?'

'Nothing,' I say. 'Did you see that? With Jess?'

'Yes, I couldn't miss it.' He looks around. 'But where are you taking me?'

'The box. It's more private there.'

'Oh?' He hesitates. Then he nudges me. 'Isn't it *complicated*?'

Oh, that. 'Yeah, whatever. Shut up.' Well, I only have about another half-hour with him anyway, at most. I don't want to waste it on his insecurity. 'I wanted to ask you something.'

Drew looks affronted. 'Well, don't expect an answer, seeing as I'm shutting up at your request.'

He's infuriating! Doesn't he realize our minutes are numbered?

Um, no. Of course he doesn't.

'Yeah, very funny,' I say. 'But listen – should we be worried about Jess? Should we let her do that? All that dancing and swishing and . . . you know. Questing. One wild dance to rule them all.'

Drew stops being annoying and considers it seriously. 'I don't know. She seems to be enjoying herself. And it isn't exactly a huge audience – plus they all looked a bit . . . coupled up. Not really paying attention.' His eyebrows waggle. Then he sighs. 'It's all my fault, anyway.'

'How do you work that out?' It's all George's fault really – and mine.

'Well, she's snapped, hasn't she? I know she's had some . . . issues since I came to live with her family, and maybe—'

'Hold on – issues? Jess has *issues*?' Jess's only issues are of library books. Tons of them.

'Yeah. I don't think she's ever really warmed to my uncle, her stepdad, and then . . .' He shifts uncomfortably. 'Well, I came along. And I don't mean to make Jess feel bad, but Aunt Sarah's always full of, you know . . .'

I know how my mum would finish that sentence. 'No. Full of what?'

'Full of praise. For me. Because I help out, even though I have my own reasons for it. I . . . I think Jess is put out. She's been trying to prove herself or something, getting more and more—'

'Obsessive about her schoolwork,' I finish for him. I

am an idiot for not noticing what my friend was going through. She's been *jealous* of Drew! Unbelievable! And yet sort of not. She's never been comfortable with the whole step-family thing. At her mum's wedding she was so sulky she wouldn't even gossip and giggle with me and Gemma. When Gemma got her third terrible stepdad, Jess was sympathizing with her far more than she should have done considering her own stepdad was utterly lovely.

'Exactly.' Drew sighs. 'Sorry, you must know all this. In fact, you probably hear the other side of it all. I know you and Jess are close.'

No, not really. We *were* close. Now I am a terrible friend who only sees things from my own point of view. I am a selfish friend who thought Jess had abandoned me, when really she needed my help.

'She's probably said some awful things about me,' Drew goes on.

'Er . . . she calls you a loser sometimes. Mostly she just rolls her eyes a lot at the slightest mention of your name.'

He laughs sadly. 'Lex, I love the way you never sugar-coat things. You always speak your mind.' He shifts on the stair. Then he puts his arms around me.

We sit like that for a while. A slight draught blows up the stairwell and tickles past us. Time stops.

'In fact, I love spending time with you full stop. I don't care if it's complicated. I want . . .'

Oh God, *I* want too.

I can't stop myself. As George would say, I'm not shy. It's just not my style. And Drew is gorgeous, and he's there, and he's looking at me in that amazing way, making me wish we were in the Adventure Tree, rolling in the romantic leaves.

I kiss him.

His arms tighten around me as he kisses me back, immediately warm and sweet. My insides stir. I kiss him deeper and longer, and our mouths blend, radiating heat until I am lost in him, ravenous. I wish this could go on for ever. My head spins.

My head spins and my phone vibrates in my pocket.

My phone vibrates in my pocket.

I can tell from the alert that it's not the alarm I set for midnight, though. It's a text message; a false alarm. I try to ignore it. I want to kiss Drew, not read some message that's probably my mum asking where I am. I pull him closer.

And then my phone vibrates again, for longer. This is it. This time it's definitely the signal I've started dreading – the one that tells me it's all over. But Drew is still kissing me.

The alarm stops. Another text message comes in but I can't think about that now. I know it's past midnight. What's going to happen? Will Jess suddenly stop interpretive dancing? Will George break away from

227

whichever girl he's with right now? Even if it's – *shudder* – Gemma? What are Lia and Tia – and Cam and Hayden, for that matter – going to think when they find themselves in the arms of someone they didn't really choose to be with?

When will Drew stop kissing me?

What have George and I done?

This is a disaster.

I don't want Drew to stop wanting me, but I know it has to happen, and I brought this heartache on myself. I should never have tried to change him. George and I shouldn't have tried to change anyone, and we deserve everything we get.

Drew keeps kissing me, grasping now because I've pulled away slightly, because I know it can't last. His kiss might be lingering, but I know that, in the long term, it's over.

I break away. A clean break. Like pulling off a plaster in one swift rip to minimize the pain.

Ouch.

Drew reaches for me. He strokes my face and caresses my hair.

I shiver – maybe the game hasn't worn off after all? – until I realize what he's doing. And why.

He touches the ends of my hair. The shortened ends – the way they were before. My hair is shorter and my clumpy bald patch is back.

It's past midnight and Cinderella's back in rags.

Drew looks confused. 'Lex, what happened to your hair? That's weird!'

I think quickly. 'I had, er ... dissolving hair extensions,' I improvise.

'Oh. I've never heard of those.'

He doesn't stop playing with my hair, rubbing strands through his fingers. It feels so nice. I never used to let Matt touch my hair. Especially not around my ears. Ever.

Then he pushes a lock behind my left ear.

He looks at me. Drew looks at my ear, not covered by hair the way I always make sure I wear it. Mum persuaded me to cut it over a year ago and I never should have agreed to that, but it was already growing out when Drew joined our school. He's never seen it properly short. The longer it is, the better I can hide. It's been wonderful having longer hair this week, especially when I was in the Adventure Tree with Drew.

The longer my hair is, the more I can pretend to be someone I'm not.

I can't look at him any more. Can't look, can't look. I don't know what he's saying.

I don't know what he's saying until he touches my shoulders softly and shifts around on the step a bit, positioning himself directly in front of me, the way all my friends do – the ones who've known me for ever; the ones who had to adjust to my new life at the same time as I did; the ones who made me feel normal until some of them, like Gemma and Matt, let me down. In style.

Drew does this instinctively even though I've never explained it to him; I've never given him lessons like I have the others. Drew is wonderful. He even takes my hands in his, which makes my heart beat faster. But I know he doesn't want to kiss me any more.

'Lex, I didn't know you wore a hearing aid,' he says, and I wish I could stop myself lip-reading those words, but years of practice has got me skilfully interpreting everyone's mouth movements and I can't help it.

I refuse to look him in the eye, though. I refuse to see what he thinks of me now; now that the game has worn off and he knows the truth.

'I don't always wear it,' I tell him. 'It doesn't work all that well for me, to be honest, and sometimes it's just annoying. I mostly rely on reading people's lips.'

'Oh, so—'

I know what he's about to ask me. 'Yes, I have a serious hearing impairment. I had meningitis when I was eleven and this was the result. It was a big change, but I adjusted. I'm a lip-reading champion. It's really no big deal.' This is a lie. It *is* a big deal, mostly because other people *make* it a big deal. 'Not everyone adjusted all that well, though,' I say more honestly.

He's still listening, still holding my hands, so I carry on. He may as well hear it all now.

'The worst one is Mum. She hates me being like this. She wants me to get a cochlear implant. It's like a bionic ear – I'd need an operation.' I pull at my hair, hiding my ears again. 'People get different results with them. It might not even work for me, but Mum says I should try it. She loves plastic surgery, and she wants me back to normal.'

Drew looks like he doesn't know what to say.

'But the worst of it is that she blamed George's dad for what happened – and I really like George's dad! It wasn't his fault. Mum was going out with him before, but they barely talk now and it's all because of me. I was sleeping over at George's house, and Martin was look-ing after me while Mum was at work, and he just thought I had flu. Besides, I've found out he's got a hospital phobia and . . . I think it was hard for him. Anyway, it's unfair because Mum's got medical training and Martin obviously hasn't, and he just didn't spot the signs, not right away. But it doesn't make any difference – Mum can't forgive him. She blames Martin for making me Special Needs.' I am rambling. I should shut up.

I don't want to. 'Mum's not the only one who's had trouble dealing with this, though. Do you want to hear more?' I don't leave Drew a gap to answer. 'There's Matt and Gemma, for example. Well, I know what we both think of Matt now, but I used to think he was my friend – and more – but it turns out he felt sorry for me and showed it by snogging me – a lot – and Gemma got jealous because she's always had a thing for Matt, and . . .' I realize something. 'And anyway, Gemma's just generally jealous of the special attention I get some-times.' I take a breath. I'm worn out. 'I don't even *want* any special attention. I don't. Not even from Mr Trench and Ms Cosgrove. But I keep getting it.'

Drew's eyes are on fire now, like that day at the tree when I told him I was thick. 'Lex, you have a hearing impairment. There's nothing wrong with getting help. It doesn't mean you—'

This tilts me fully into rant mode. 'Are you going to tell me that being practically deaf doesn't mean I can't do everything other people do? Because I agree with you – in fact, I barely even admit to myself that I'm different from anyone else. Because I'm not, am I?' I swallow hard. 'I just can't hear very well. But if I'm the same as everyone else, then why do I have so much trouble concentrating in lessons, and why am I so rubbish at everything?' I shrug, winding down now, not meeting Drew's eyes.

'Lex . . .' He puts his hands back on my shoulders – my friends' usual signal that they want to tell me some-thing. But I don't want to know what Drew has to say, so I don't look at him. I haven't finished what I was say-ing myself.

'The only explanation is that I'm stupid, Drew. No

matter what Mr Trench is told to say with his SENCO training, no matter how many film courses he sends me on to boost my confidence and emphasize my "different abilities", as he puts it. So, you know. You didn't believe me before, when I told you in the forest . . .' In fact, he said all those wonderful things, but I need to forget that. 'But that's the truth about me.'

After that, I remember to breathe.

Drew shakes his head and doesn't let go of my shoulders. 'It's not right that you feel this way, Lex. I mean it. You should talk to someone about it. There's a whole community out there . . . People who've been through what you have. They could help you talk things through.'

Now he sounds like my mother. She's always trying to get me to go to 'special' youth clubs and groups she finds out about through her work. Half the reason I agreed to the film course was that her suggested alternative was a 'special' activity week for 'special' people like me.

I want Drew to think I'm special, but not in *that* way. I don't want Drew to sound like my mother. I want him to kiss me senseless in the Adventure Tree.

But the spell's worn off now.

Drew's still talking, having a monologue of his own now. 'I have a good pal back home who's Deaf – you know, with a capital D. He's part of the Deaf community. You should meet him, Lex – he's such a laugh and I really think you'd get on with him . . .'

I look away, because now he's trying to fix me up with someone else, someone 'like me', and I've had enough.

Game over. For ever.

I shrug away from Drew's hold and shout the worst words I can think of to tell him to get lost because, right this second, I can't stand him. I can't believe he tried to do that to me. He's as bad as Matt, feeling sorry for me. I hate Drew for this. I *hate* him!

I rush for the emergency exit, pushing the bar down hard and not looking back. Then I run down the High Street, past the park where Jess spent her rebel morning, and up to the station, which is closed at this time of night in our sleepy town. Even the taxi rank looks quiet – not that I have enough money for one anyway. But I bet most of the cabs are now parked outside the clubs I was at with Drew earlier, when things were so different.

I stop and gasp for breath, more out of a weird grief for Drew than because of the running. It's over. It's over, and I never want to see him again.

But how am I going to get home now?

I pull out my phone. There's only one option. He's probably awake at his computer, just like his son used to be before this crazy week. He can cover for me with Mum too. She might not even ask questions, not if I turn up with him.

I know Martin won't mind.

There are two unread texts on my phone – they must be the ones that came in earlier, either side of my alarm. I can see that they're from Gemma but I don't want to read whatever nasty things she has to say to me, not while I'm feeling like this – all chewed up.

I bypass the messages to text Martin.

I picture him arriving in his sensible dad-car. I can tell him where George is too, in case he's wondering. Though maybe Martin won't even remember that George went out.

My heart goes out to George, who's been a brilliant friend to me for years, and never once let me down, not in a way that matters – not like the others. My earlier feelings of anger towards him completely disappear as I think about how lost he is beneath his solid, nerdy exterior. He didn't mean to cause the trouble he caused, any more than I did. George is just mixed up and kind of lonely. He could do with more attention from his dad, actually. Maybe I'll tell Martin that too, when he does the dad-thing and takes me home. Maybe I'll ask to stick around and sleep over like I used to when I was younger, and then I can give George the hug I think he needs.

Within minutes, my phone vibrates. I read the latest message first – the one from Martin saying he's on his way like the reliable dad-type I know he is. If only Mum would forgive him. I've wanted that to happen for years.

With that thought, I feel strong enough to open the previous two texts – the ones from Gemma.

There's one she sent just before midnight that says: Changed settings on ur crazy game when u left the room so that u LUV George!!! In 1 minute! Just 2 spook u out cos u believe it + then I can get him 1st! Ha HA!

And then, just after midnight: Weird — I don't even care about him at all any more. Going to find Matty. George is ALL YOURS now!! Loads of LUV!! G xx.

PART THREE:

love

I don't get much time to think about Gemma's texts before Martin pulls up and I instantly stop wishing he was my dad.

He has Mum in the passenger seat!

I don't believe it. All this time I've been dying for them to spend more time together, and the one time they do is when I desperately don't want them to! Why has he brought her? What part of 'Here's where I am, please come and get me' means 'And bring my mother, who's already seriously annoyed with me'?

She gives me one of her looks. 'Get in,' she says through gritted teeth. She doesn't have to add, 'You're in big trouble, Lex.'

No one tries to talk to me on the way home. I focus on beaming evils at the backs of their heads.

I also start to worry about what Gemma wrote. Is that why she gave me such a horrible smirk as she was leaving George's house? Has she really changed my settings to make me love George? Because, if she has, then this is it. We can't change the game now. Everything was supposed to be set back to normal. What am I going to do?

I sit back and consider my feelings for George. I'm not sure what I think. Tonight was all too much – I'm completely confused. But is this a part of it, all the confusion? Is this how Gemma felt? Is this how Matt and Drew felt when they thought about me in the last couple of days?

I think about Drew. I wish I was still in Drew's arms. But Drew isn't interested in me any more, no matter what George said before about using the game to help us. Why else was one of the first things Drew said to me after midnight an attempt to fix me up with one of his friends? No, it's over for me and Drew.

Do I love George now?

My thoughts keep churning all the way home, so that by the time Martin pulls into our road, I've almost forgotten that I have to face the wrath of Mum in a minute. Maybe I should just throw myself at her feet and beg for forgiveness right here in the car and get it over with. It would involve climbing over the gearstick in a moving car, though, so maybe not such a good idea.

Martin parks and we get out of the car in silence. Mum stands under our intruder light, so I clearly see her thanking Martin with tight lips. She says, 'I'm sure you're grateful that your son never causes you this kind of worry.' I set my expression to 'bored' but I feel like shouting at her.

Martin gives his trademark puzzled look. 'Actually, Fiona . . .'

He hasn't called Mum that for years. He's avoided calling her anything at all, really. Mum's noticed it too, and she does a bit of a double-take.

'I didn't like to mention it before, but I'm not too sure where George is right now. He had a . . . bit of a party at our house earlier.'

Mum looks shocked.

'Then he went out . . . to a disco or something? With, ahem . . . a few girls. And a couple of boys.'

Mum seems marginally less shocked for a second, until it sinks in that this is George we're talking about, and then she seems more shocked.

Martin gives me an apologetic look. 'I know you were with that tough-looking pierced boy after George left, but do you happen to know where he is, Lex?'

That's how Mum, Martin and I end up sitting around the kitchen table of George's house, among the debris of the earlier party, staring at each other in silence.

Mum goes first. 'Well, Lex? Where have you been tonight, and who's this pierced boy Martin's talking about? And don't try to tell me you've been with Jess because I'm not falling for that one again.'

That's a laugh, considering I *was* with Jess, a bit. I pick up the teapot Jess sashayed around earlier and fiddle with its spotty design.

'Well?' Mum repeats. 'I want to hear everything.'

I shrug, which I know will get her back up, but I can't help it. The situation completely calls for a shrug. 'I was out at the chippy with Matt.' Wow, that feels like a long time ago. 'Then I was here at George's house with . . . well, mostly everyone from the film course. Including Jess's cousin – he's the boy Martin mentioned. And then . . .' I decide to skip the parts with Drew in the car, because we were basically on the way to our final destination. Plus I don't think Mum approves of Drew, thanks to the way Martin has introduced him. 'Then at the Bijou. With everyone. I left . . . everyone there. That's where George probably still is.'

I still wonder what happened when the clock struck midnight, though. I wonder how everyone's coping with the fallout from the game.

Mum stands up, adjusting her jacket. 'Then we should go and get him,' she says. She hesitates when no one else moves. 'Martin? Aren't you coming?'

Martin goes a bit red in the face. 'Um . . . steady on, Fiona.' Sometimes I can really see where George gets his old-fashioned way of speaking. 'My son's nearly seventeen and he's at his favourite cinema.'

'Mike put *The Fellowship of the Ring* on really late,' I

add, which earns me a sharp look from Mum. 'What? He did.'

'You spend far too much time at that flea-pit too, Lex.'

I'm guessing the 'too' is because she's thinking I spend too much time at George's house, but she won't say it in front of Martin. I roll my eyes.

'Now, Fiona, I know George and Lex love that place and I'm sure it's perfectly clean.'

Mum gives an exasperated sigh. 'OK, maybe he's at the cinema, but do you know all the people he's with?' I'm not even sure whether she's addressing me or George's dad. 'How can you be sure they're not trouble-makers—'

I can't believe Martin actually interrupts her. 'No, I don't know them, and I can't be sure. But I trust him. I trust my son.'

Mum sits down heavily, like she's kind of deflating. Her eyes go shiny. 'Are you implying I don't trust my daughter?'

'Oh, Fiona . . .' Martin blusters. 'Of course not.'

They both look at me.

Now I want to disappear. Or spring to Mum's defence, because much as I love Martin, watching his face crease with worry doesn't have the same effect on me as seeing Mum close to tears like she is now.

Her tearful look is mixed with this careful dignity she always has, though. She literally holds her head high when she says, 'You'll never understand the difficulties I've had to cope with, Martin. You'll never know how hard it is to watch your child's life completely change, almost *overnight*.'

I glare at her, but suddenly, when it matters, neither of them seems to be looking at me any more.

They start to squabble in short, tense exchanges that contain polite words but are delivered with the backing of years of grudge-bearing (Mum) and guilt (Martin) and confusion (both of them).

I put the teapot down calmly. I am calm. I am. I just can't take it any more. That's all.

'Stop it!' I yell, even though shouting gives me a low-frequency buzzing sensation I hate. I'm prepared to suffer for this, though. I have truly had enough. 'Stop it, stop it, stop it, and listen to ME for a change!'

They both go quiet, exchanging a quick look with each other before they stare at me. Mum doesn't seem like she wants to tell me off for once, and Martin doesn't seem like he wants to pat me on the head and send me up to George's room. I have the attention of both of them. At last.

'I'm sick of this. I'm sick of the way you are with Martin, Mum. And I'm sick of the way you allow it, Martin,' I add quickly, in case he gets any ideas and starts getting smug. They're in this together, really, and they're as bad as each other.

'Lex,' Mum starts, but I interrupt her immediately.

'Listen! To! Me!' I take a deep breath. 'I don't care if you two fight about things that have nothing to do with me. Believe me, I don't even want to *know* about that stuff. But if you're going to dredge up things that happened to *me* as a reason to fight, or not talk, or whatever, then you need to listen to me.'

'Lex—'

'You need to hear this, Mum. So Martin didn't get me to hospital all that quickly that night when I was eleven – so what? What if I'd been with Nan that night, and she'd just assumed I had flu? Would you have blanked *her* for ever?' I continue quickly because maybe she would, I don't know. 'What if you'd been home yourself, but exhausted and busy watching one of your programmes? It could have happened.'

'Lex—'

'It *could* have happened, Mum. The fact is, I'm here. Martin *did* get me to hospital in the end and I'm fine. I'm alive! My life has just changed a bit. That's all. It's not a bad thing, it's just a *thing*. One of those things. Everyone has them. George is socially challenged, Jess is obsessive, Gemma's a jealous cow—'

'Lex!'

Yeah, OK, that last one didn't quite fit. 'It doesn't make me love them any less.' Even Gemma, in some ways. It's hard to end a friendship when you've known

245

someone all your life, when you've been through so much with them. Maybe I can love and hate her at the same time.

'All I'm saying is that I'm not *damaged*. I'm just me. And Mum, if you're going to keep getting at Martin about it, then it makes me think . . .' I gulp. 'It makes me think you're ashamed of me. That you'd rather have me back the way I was before it happened. Undamaged.'

'No, Lex . . .' Mum's eyes are brimming now, and it makes me feel heartless, but I can't stop – not now. She has to hear this.

'You're not helping me, Mum. I'm struggling at school, I feel stupid because I can't keep up, and seeing you have a go at Martin for *making* me this way isn't helping me feel . . .' I think about what Drew said. I realize he's right. 'Isn't helping me feel like I'm someone who just happens to need extra help occasionally. It makes me feel like a burden – like I should hide my disability and pretend to be normal.' Like I did with Drew, when I probably shouldn't have. 'Which is ridiculous because *no one* is normal anyway.'

A wave of exhaustion hits me. It's been a strange night.

'So . . . I know some of this is my problem, and I'll work on it. But you two need to get your act together too. And that's all I'm saying.'

I fold my arms on the kitchen table and slump down into them.

246

Mum gets up and hugs what she can reach of me, sniffing into my hair, while Martin hovers awkwardly beside us.

I don't exactly hear the phone ring but I sense Mum reacting, so I'm not surprised when I look up and see Martin mumbling, 'Shall I get that?' and Mum nodding.

He walks out for a minute and then comes back with a grey face.

'That was the, er, police,' he says. 'George has been taken in on suspicion of breaking and entering, over at the film course headquarters.' He clears his throat. 'The police investigated when they saw a light on in the hut after midnight. It seems George was there with a – ahem – girl. I'm sorry, but I think I need to get to the police station.'

'We're coming with you,' I announce.

Martin heads for the door in a daze. 'You were right, Fiona.'

Mum catches up with him and puts a firm hand on his shoulder.

George's plans for relieving his guilt – both about the game and about breaking his toe and delaying the progress of the film course – kind of backfired on him. It turns out that's what he was trying to do last night. He wasn't having a party – he'd actually invited everyone from the film course over to his house to

247

discuss how to get the course back on track. Poor George. He honestly thought our friends would turn up at a house with access to drink, sound equipment and an almost total lack of parental supervision, and they'd just sit around talking about coursework. He will never understand that he's one-of-a-kind.

Anyway, he did get all the film course members to come to his house – even me and Drew, eventually – so at least he didn't totally fail. But he soon worked out that all they were going to do was party, snog each other, try to lure him up to his bedroom under false pretences and/or dance a lot before deciding to go clubbing and ending up in the cinema.

He was at the Bijou when midnight struck and everything went slowly into meltdown. Lia and Tia spent ages loudly dumping Cam and Hayden, Jess slunk off the stage and into the audience in a stupor – until Drew found her and took her home, Gemma stood in the foyer madly texting Matt, I'd already shouted at Drew in the stairwell and legged it, and George . . . quietly watched the film for a couple of minutes before deciding to abandon the mess he'd created. He thought he would take a taxi up to Base Camp Har Har and finish the film by himself. He wanted to try and make *something* right.

Someone went with him, though – the girl that George had apparently been trying to resist snogging all week. The 'real girl' he mentioned to me earlier, who made him decide he didn't want Jess any more. And it was just as well she followed George, because it was nearly all down to her that he didn't actually get arrested.

The girl was Kathryn, and the reason she helped was that – with a short taxi detour – she had access to the Base Camp Har Har keys. This meant there was no actual 'breaking and entering' – which apparently my closet-rebel friend George was actually considering, because he felt so strongly about getting the film ready. But thanks to Kathryn and the keys she sneaked out of her mother's handbag, there was just a possible trespassing charge. Even that couldn't really stick after Ms Cosgrove arrived at the police station to collect her daughter and make a good case for the release of the Har Har Two.

Because it turns out that Kathryn Ellison is Ms Cosgrove's daughter, who landed up at our school after her parents got divorced and her mother could no longer afford her private school fees. Kathryn didn't want anyone to know she was related to a teacher – she's shy enough as it is – and the Cosmic One agreed to keep it quiet.

Well, her secret's safe with me . . . for now. If she doesn't treat George right, I totally have something on her.

I also have a feeling that those lingering effects of the

game – the ones George was talking about – might have worked on her in a way they didn't on Drew. I got this from the way Kathryn and George looked at each other when we all said goodbye outside the police station and went our separate ways. And also from the way they were eating each other's faces off when the policeman opened the interview-room door to release them – something Ms Cosgrove found very embarrassing and my mother found very surprising. (When will Mum ever learn to listen to me?)

George tells me all this – well, the bits I didn't already witness myself – when we're home, in *my* house this time, and Mum and Martin have left us to chat over a cup of late-night tea and a plate of emergency Martin biscuits.

When George finishes his version of events, I give him a proper big hug, knocking his crutches to the floor in the process.

'Nice one, jailbait!' I say. I ruffle his hair.

He yawns. 'Jail*bird*, Lex. Jailbait means something different. I'm sixteen. I'm legal.'

'You *wish*.' I nudge him.

He gives me a feeble smile.

I think about Gemma's last-minute change to the game and decide it's time to confess my true feelings for George.

'Hey, George, by the way ...' I flick his shoulder.

'I love you.' Well, it's true, game-induced or not.

He shakes his head. 'You're impossible.'

'No, seriously. I do.' I smile. 'What's wrong?'

'I don't know, Lex. I just thought the first time a girl said she loved me would be a bit more . . . you know. Passionate.' He shrugs. 'More hearts and flowers. Fewer clothes.'

'Oh. God, you're soppy. And sick.' I give him another hug, though this time with slightly less bodily contact. 'I really do love you, George. Besides, you're stuck with me now. Gemma changed the settings of the game. I'm set to love you for ever. We're going to have to get used to it, like an arranged marriage.'

'At least you've stopped calling me your brother.' He sighs. 'Wait a minute. *Gemma* knew about the game? Did she know how to re-activate it?'

'I showed her how to change the settings. In your room. When she came up to taunt me about how, in our mutual quest to win your luscious lips, she was going to get you first.'

He perks up. 'You were mutually questing to win my luscious lips?'

'Gemma thought we were.'

'Jess actually sent her up to tell you we were all going clubbing. She saw you go up there when she leaped off the table at the end of her macarena. Then she was in too much of a dance-induced rush to wait for you, and we all rushed after her. We were a bit scared for her.'

I give him a sideways look. 'Who's *we*?'

'Everyone.' He smiles. 'Though especially me and Kathryn. We'd been talking for most of the night. Apart from when Gemma asked to see my poster . . . But I told you nothing was going on with Gemma.'

I raise my eyebrows. 'But something was going on with Kathryn? What did *she* think you were doing upstairs with Gemma?'

'Nothing. Because that's the truth. Kathryn knows how I feel about her.'

'George!' I give him a shove. 'I should be very jealous of this Kathryn, you know. By the law of *Pygmalions*, you are *mine*!'

George groans.

'Oh, thanks a *lot*,' I say. 'I thought the first time I told a boy I loved him and he belonged to me he'd, you know . . . be a tiny bit happy about it.'

'That's not what I'm groaning about. You can love me for ever, I don't mind. Though I might still be looking for the other kind of love.'

'The clothes-off kind?'

'With or without the invisibility cloak.' His eyes cloud with soppiness. 'Kathryn loves *Harry Potter*. And *Lord of the Rings*. And gaming. She's a *World of Warcraft* level thirty-nine.' His smile spreads. 'And she likes me.'

'Get *out*! Or rather – get *in*! That's brilliant, George.

Who'd have expected that from a Child of the Cosmos!' I ponder the horror of having a parent who's a teacher at school – then I think about the potential gossip a girl like Kathryn could get hold of. Not least . . . 'So is there anything going on between Mr Trench and Kathryn's mum?'

George looks shocked. 'No way! What makes you think that? Oh my God – Kathryn would hate that. She wants her parents to get back together. Besides, she can't stand Mr Trench.'

'So? You don't get to choose your step-parents.' I think of Mum and Martin. I wonder whether they'll patch things up now. I'm thinking probably not, although they already seem a bit friendlier to each other, and Mum should stop having a go at me about seeing George from now on.

Then I consider the fact that Mum and Martin's relationship is probably none of my business anyway. But I don't really believe that. 'Hey, maybe you should ask your dad to speak to the people who invented *Pygmalions*. Maybe they could develop a *Choose Your Own Parent* game. Isn't that a brilliant idea?'

George shakes his head. 'Lex, do you never learn?'

I grin. 'Anyway, you can't complain – the game really worked out for you!'

He groans. 'I hate that game. We should never have started tinkering with people's lives. It was completely wrong, what we did, and it was a huge headache and I'm never trying to change anyone ever again.'

'That's rich, coming from someone who got a girl-friend out of it.' I remember Thursday night. 'Oh, and someone who forgot to wipe off the settings before he went on an all-night crime spree, so we all very nearly stayed like that for ever. It's a good thing I *did* sneak up to your room during your weird party so I could set everything back to normal.' I kick him affectionately on the shins. 'Except Gemma's setting, of course, my beloved.'

George is unmoved by my heroism and/or devotion. 'No, I de-activated the game before you got there,' he tells me. 'We still had to wait until midnight to get back to normal, but it was sorted, I promise.'

I shake my head. 'The settings definitely weren't changed back. I spent ages on it.'

'Ah,' says George. 'That's because I didn't wipe the settings. I de-activated the game altogether. I figured it out.' He looks smug.

'Figured what out?'

'I figured out how we activated the Pygmas in the first place, and I reversed the process.'

'In English?'

'I deleted the dates of birth from all the profiles, Lex. Don't ask me how, but that's what was making the Pygmas work. The correct dates of birth set the game off, so deleting them stopped everything after mid-night.' He picks at a biscuit and goes suddenly shy. 'That's how I knew Kathryn wasn't like the others. We didn't know her birthday. She was never under the influence of the game.' He gives a little smile. 'She *really* liked me all along.'

'Oh my God, George! Seriously? Hold on. Are you sure? How did you work it out?'

He puts his hand in front of his mouth when he replies.

I pull it away, grab his other hand too, and hold them behind his back.

'Ow, Lex, you're hurting me!'

'Suffer, my sweet love! Tell me how you worked it out.'

'Dad found a manual in an old jiffy bag. I—'

'You read the manual! You read the *manual*!' I do an almost Jess-like dance around the kitchen. I open the kitchen window and shout out, 'People of our street! George read the manual! And because of that, I don't have to love him for ever, but I think I will anyway, just to annoy him!'

'Lex! I take it back. I'm not going to *let* you love me for ever now.'

'You don't get a say in it – manual-reader!'

Mum and Martin come in and tell us to keep the noise down because we have other neighbours and it's time to go to bed after our ordeal. They're not wrong, either. It has been the craziest day of my life.

It's only when George has gone and I'm up in my room that it occurs to me.

We didn't have Drew's date of birth either.

Drew was never under the influence of the game either.

The last day of the film course starts far too early. Everyone is slumped in their chairs, exhausted – even Ms Cosgrove, who was at the police station with us only about five hours ago, after all.

There's also a subdued air of post-game trauma. Cam and Hayden exchange brief words because their dates suddenly bailed on them last night – though they seem to recover pretty quickly when they discuss the finer points of the *Lord of the Rings* trilogy instead. Lia and Tia seem a bit shell-shocked, but after a while I realize they're discussing other boys from school, and I lip-read Lia saying, 'I've never been interested in a guy for that long – it was over two days! Freaky.' I think they're going to be OK.

Jess is snoozing, too tired to speak to me, and Gemma won't meet my eyes at all. She has her phone out and is texting at every opportunity – probably making up for lost time with Matt after the Couple of the Century had a few game-induced days apart.

Drew isn't here. I try not to think about it. I remind

myself that he was supposed to be working last night, and maybe he went straight there after the craziness at the Bijou. I wonder about prodding Jess awake to ask her, but I'm even more sure now that she'd be furious with me if she knew I had a thing for her cousin.

And I really, seriously *do* have a thing for her cousin. But who knows what he'll think of me after last night. He might not have been under the influence of the game, but that doesn't mean he'll ever want to speak to me again after I walked out on him like that.

Not to mention the reason I shouted at him in the first place – the fact that he was trying to fix me up with his friend, just because we're both deaf.

Mr Trench comes bounding in, breaking through our general apathy with his newfound upbeat attitude. I think, out of everyone on this course, he might possibly have changed the most. It's weird how it's not always the obvious things that change us. As far as I can see, Mr Trench owes his current happiness to the belief that two of his SEN students have got a little something out of one of his courses. It must be an easy life of pleasure, being a teacher.

It turns out that George and Kathryn actually managed to get quite a bit of film stuff done last night, as well as . . . whatever else they were up to when the police arrived. They found they could get through the editing a lot quicker without Ms Cosgrove's interruptions, and they set some of the rendering to run overnight, which Ms Cosgrove didn't realize you could do. Thanks to them, we're almost up to date now on what we need to do for tonight. Ms Cosgrove should really be happy that her daughter was instrumental in saving the course and giving the Bijou a night to remember – the second in a row.

Instead, though, the Cosmic One keeps frowning at George, no doubt re-living last night's brush with the long arm of the law. Before this week I would have found it impossible to imagine George being seen by someone's mum as a bad influence on their daughter. I feel like high-fiving my beloved friend for his un-expected bad-boy prowess.

We work as a group on a few finishing touches, and then Mr Trench says he has to leave some processes to run by themselves for a while, and announces that we can have an extra-long lunch break because 'a watched film never renders, ha ha ha'. This is his idea of film-making wit.

He encourages us, Cosmic-like, to 'have a walk in the forest and get some fresh air' because 'tonight will be a challenging experience'. News of last night obviously hasn't reached his delicate Trench ears.

I wonder about going to the Adventure Tree and wait-ing for Drew. Maybe if he turns up, I can talk to him – I can try to find out whether I was over-reacting last night. But I'm not sure. I'm almost scared to – what if I was right and he really *did* go off me the minute he found out the truth? Besides, why would he even turn up? What if I sit there by myself for an hour, rolling in the leaves and clutching my heart?

Jess is propping up a tree near the hut, her eyes closed. If she wasn't wearing jeans, she'd look exactly like Alice in Wonderland, right down to the hairband and the glossy straight hair.

I walk over and she opens her eyes.

'Lex, my long-lost friend,' she says.

Oh, I miss her so much! I miss Gemma too. But I think I've lost Gemma and I haven't lost Jess – not yet. I make up my mind not to get back with Drew whatever happens, even though it's unlikely anyway: Jess wouldn't like it, and Jess is worth more to me than any boy. I'll just have to get over Drew as quickly as possible.

'Hey, Jess.' I flop down on the grass opposite her. 'Um, sorry about last night.' As soon as I say it, I wonder how I'm going to explain *why* I'm sorry.

She smiles. 'I had a brilliant time. It's made me remember how much I love dancing.' She does a lazy little upper-body dance. 'I'm taking it up again, Lex. I should have time for that and exam stuff, shouldn't I?'

I nod. 'Yeah. Why not?'

She sighs. 'I've gone a bit crazy lately, haven't I? I'm really sorry, Lex. I've been . . . dealing with some stuff.'

I settle down and wait for her to share her feelings about her mum and stepdad – and Drew. I prepare for the conversation we should have had weeks ago, if I'd made more of an effort with her instead of letting her push me away.

Instead she looks into the distance, where George and Kathryn are holding hands and walking through the woods. Well, Kathryn is walking and George is hobbling, but still. He doesn't have his crutches today and I suppose his toe is getting better – or his luurve is holding him up. It wasn't very long ago that me and George were spying on Jess working with Kathryn in the exact spot he's just reached. It's weird how much things have changed.

Jess sighs and says, 'It's going to be strange not having George worshipping me.'

'Jess!' I laugh. 'I didn't even think you'd noticed.'

'In the last – what? Ten years? I couldn't exactly avoid it. I just didn't want to encourage him. Only now I think I'm going to miss it. He's sweet.'

I give her a stern look. 'But you don't approve of secondary school trysts.'

'I absolutely don't,' she confirms. She goes all shifty. 'Anyway, George is nice, but he's not my type.'

Something about her expression makes me ask, 'OK, who is he – this guy who's your type?'

She sits up. 'What makes you think . . . ?' Then she leans

back. 'I thought you'd never ask.' Her eyes are determined. Defiant, even. 'Then again, I'm never telling you. It was just a crush. A very stupid crush, and I'm over it now, and it's way too embarrassing to dredge up. Ever.'

'Who? Whoooooo?'

'You sound like an owl.'

'Yeah, well, I'm going to *swoop* if you don't tell me.'

'You're going to kill me if I do. That's partly why I've been, um, avoiding you a bit.' Her eyes cloud. 'I'm sorry, Lex.'

I don't care! I want gossip! 'Jess, just tell me who you had a crush on!'

She gives me a long look. 'Swear you won't tell anyone? Especially not Gemma?'

'Why not Gemma?' An awful thought hits me. 'Oh no, Jess, please tell me you weren't crushing on Matt!' Nooooo! First George enjoying the attention from Gemma, and now this?

'Of course it wasn't Matt! I don't know what Gemma sees in him.' She bites her lip. 'I don't know what *you* saw in him either. Even after you split up.'

'I didn't—'

'You told me you were seeing him again.'

Oh. That. 'Well, I'm not, and I never will be.'

She nods. 'Yeah, I didn't think so. So does that mean you'll finally stop fighting with Gemma over him?'

'I've never—'

'Lex, come on, I'm not stupid. I know what's been going on between you and Gemma. That's why I sent her up to get you last night – I was hoping you'd get a chance to talk and maybe sort things out. You didn't, though, did you? And you have to tell me every last detail sometime. You have to stop shutting me out, pretending everything's OK.'

'OK. But you're one to talk.' I think we've all been rubbish this year. But right now I really want to know this: 'So you definitely didn't have a crush on Matt?'

'No! Lex! God.'

'So why don't you want Gemma to know?'

'Because there's no way she'd understand.' She gives a little grin. 'She'd be even worse than you.'

'What do you mean? I'm supportive and entirely non-judgemental.' I'm also dying to know. 'So tell me now, you annoying tease!'

Jess looks sceptical, but she takes a deep breath and says quickly, 'OK. You swear . . . ?'

'Yes!'

'It was . . . it was Mr Trench.' She winces. 'I suddenly got this big crush on him. It started during one of my Gifted and Talented sessions, when he was being all attentive and . . . mature. Like he was interested in my *mind*, you know. Not like the boys at school.'

I can't help myself. 'Mr Trench? Sir TRENCH of FOOT?' I shudder, and I'm probably booming like a proper Trenchie myself now. 'Oh my GOD, Jess, no WAY! Urrrgh!'

'Well, thanks for your non-judgemental support. Anyway, it was a stupid crush, like I said. No one knew – especially not him. Thank God. I was so desperate to impress him all the time, Lex! I was going crazy trying to be a model student because I know he likes that sort of thing. You know how much he adores the Gifted and Talented group.'

He seems to quite like the Improvers now too, I think.

'And I thought I was so much more grown up than the rest of you . . . I thought I was above it all, I suppose, and I stupidly thought Mr Trench might actually think I was mature enough too . . . Then last night I was just enjoying myself in a totally silly way, and it made me realize how ridiculous I was being. Like Mr Trench would ever think I was anything but a pathetic schoolgirl. Which I am.' She clutches her heart like in my film, and in her dance last night. 'Stupid crush. Ouch. I've crushed it now.'

'You're not pathetic at all,' I say. 'Just . . . misguided. I mean, honestly. Mr *Trench*?' I start babbling, partly to hide my revulsion. 'Besides, I think there might be something going on between him and Ms Cosgrove.'

Jess looks shocked. 'But they hate each other – it's obvious!'

'I bet that's what they *want* us to think. Anyway, sometimes hate is the first stage of love.'

'Lex, no. No way!'

'Oh, sorry, was that a bit insensitive of me?' I give her a sideways glance complete with smirk. 'Because you *fancy* him—'

'I told you I don't. Not any more! And I swear, if you keep teasing me about this, I will have *such* a go at you about the way you're secretly in love with my awful step-cousin.'

I go all hot and cold. *'What?* How did you . . .? Did George tell you that?' I seriously doubt it, especially given the way I've been talking about Matt to him lately, but it's the only possibility I can think of.

She looks at me. 'No, Lex. It's the most completely obvious thing in the world and it has been for ages.'

'Oh.' My heart sinks. Should I tell her I've made a mess of it all anyway? But I'm not sure I want to admit to Jess that anything actually went on between me and Drew. She'll hate me.

Jess nudges me. 'Hey, it's OK. You should go for it.' She smiles. 'After all, you can't help who you like.' I know the look she gives me then means: *So stop teasing me about Mr Trench* – but all I can think is that I want to jump up and punch the air.

'You mean you don't mind? About me and Drew?' If there *is* a 'me and Drew', but still. I was definitely expecting Jess to mind – big-time.

She shrugs. 'I think you have seriously dodgy taste . . .'

I stop myself from shouting, 'Mr *Trench*?!'

'But what sort of friend would I be if I stood in your way? Besides, it might shut him up at last. He's always going on and on about you at home, asking me all these questions.' She does a huge pretend-yawn.

'What kinds of questions?'

'Everything. What subjects you study, what films you like, how long you've been deaf—'

I gulp. 'He asked you *that*?'

'Yes.'

'When? When did he ask you?'

'I don't know . . . start of term?'

Drew knew I was deaf at the *start of term*?

'Did you answer?'

'Yes. Very briefly.'

All those times on the Chairs of Doom when I thought I had a clean slate with Drew, the boy who'd only ever met me at Jess's mum's wedding, before it happened? When a small part of me was interested in him just because I thought he didn't know; because being with Matt might have made me *feel* normal for a while, but I thought Drew really did see me as properly normal . . .

And now it turns out that Drew has known about me all along?

I immediately realize it doesn't matter. I'm actually

happy about that. I think about how 'normal' is meaningless, just like I keep telling people. I'm starting to actually believe it now, for the first time. My hearing impairment is a part of me, and Drew has always known it, and even if he hadn't . . . it doesn't make any difference.

Jess shoots me a worried look. 'Is it OK that I answered?'

'Yes, except that I thought he didn't know,' I say. 'Last night he seemed surprised when he saw my hearing aid.'

'Oh, I bet that's because of his Scottish mate – the one he keeps telling Mum about. Apparently this friend is militant about Deaf Rights and refuses to go near anything to do with audiology. Maybe Drew thought you were like him.'

'Oh. Yes, he mentioned him . . . when I told him about Mum wanting me to get cochlear implants, and how I wasn't sure about it.'

'Yeah, Drew's mate could be a good person to talk to about that kind of thing. He'll see things differently from your mum.'

'Yeah.' Which is probably what Drew meant after all.

Jess is acting casual but her eyes are wide. 'So you talked to Drew about that? And you let him see your hearing aid? Wow! You're normally so secretive about it

– always pulling your hair over your ears. I know you hate people talking about you.'

'Is that why you only answered briefly when he asked how long I'd been deaf?'

'Kind of.' Jess picks at some grass. 'Mostly it's because I only talk to him in words of one syllable or less, if I talk to him at all,' she admits. 'Um, sorry. It just drives me crazy that Mum thinks Drew is so perfect.'

It's slightly weird that I agree with Sarah Hartford about something. My mum must never find out. 'I still can't believe he knew. And you didn't tell him? Not even ages ago?'

'Definitely not.' Jess shrugs. 'Mum might have mentioned it, I suppose. Or he could have heard it around school. He was probably listening out for information about you. He's interested in you, Lex. *Very* interested. He's got it bad.' She smiles. 'And he's here.'

I jump. I turn. 'Where?'

'Not that close. He just walked past, that way.' She points into the forest, in the direction of the Adventure Tree. That thought makes my heart leap.

Jess moans, 'Mum's probably just dropped him off late again. She's all, *Oh, poor ickle disadvantaged Drew, there's no need to get up at a normal time like the rest of the human race.* It's infuriating.' She looks at me. 'Yeah, I know. I'll get over it one day. Maybe. I sort of enjoyed texting him yesterday, to be honest. And I'm sure my

267

dodgy-taste best friend will talk me round eventually.'

I throw my arms around her in a massive hug. 'God, I've missed you, Jess.'

'I've missed you too.' She gets a mischievous sparkle in her eye. 'But you should save this huggy stuff for the most annoying guy in the world.'

I hesitate until she waves me away. 'Go get him, Lex.'

I love my friends.

Talking to Jess properly at last has made me feel all relaxed and happy and like anything is possible. But every step I take towards the Adventure Tree adds another butterfly to my stomach until they form a solid mass with no room to flutter. It's like an old film I saw with George once, called *The Birds*. I've always thought birds were quite nice, but in this film they start looking menacing just because there are so many of them.

Butterflies are normally lovely, but mine are currently attacking me from the inside.

The only thing that calms me down is the thought that Drew wouldn't have gone to the Adventure Tree if he wasn't planning to meet me. And he wouldn't plan to meet me if he really believed what I shouted at him yesterday. Would he?

I reach the tree and take a deep breath.

I step between the familiar branches and into our world.

He's not there.

I sit down in the middle of our film set and stir the pile of leaves with my hands. I pick some up and throw them into the air. I just about stop short of rolling about in them, clutching my heart.

My butterflies flap away and leave me empty. I've blown it! George put the idea in my head that Drew has liked me all along, and Jess confirmed it with what she said just now, but if he's not here, it can only mean one thing: he has definitely given up on me. And I can't really blame him, can I? I told him to get lost, and I said it as harshly as I possibly could.

I can't stay here feeling like this – despite what Matt and Gemma might think, there's nothing I like *less* than feeling sorry for myself. I stand up and push the branches aside and . . . there he is. Walking towards the tree, looking slightly lost. Drew.

I want to jump up and down and pull him into the leaves, and lots more besides, but the look on his face stops me. His expressive eyebrows are flat as he reaches me. He says, 'Lex.'

'Um. Drew,' I say. I try a little smile. 'Hi. I was hoping you'd be here.'

He doesn't return the smile. 'Why? So you can play more games with me?'

My heart sinks and my first thought is, *How can he possibly know about the game?* And I feel guilty and

269

terrible, and I try to tell myself that George changed that setting, not me, but that still doesn't make it right. Then I remind myself that Drew was never affected by the game at all, and that day when I asked if he was going to kiss me – well, *cringe*, no wonder he didn't say yes. Although he did kiss me back when I kissed him and . . .

He's just looking at me. Then he says, 'I can't believe I fell for you, Lex. I feel like such an idiot.'

He fell for me! 'Why?'

'Because it doesn't make any sense. I barely know you. You never told me a thing about yourself outside Mr Trench's office. You never talked to me – not properly.'

'But you knew I was deaf.'

I think I mean it as an accusation, but he just skirts over it like it's no big deal. 'I knew a few things about you from watching you and asking around, but I wanted to know everything. And I wanted to hear it from you.'

I realize that, to him, my hearing impairment actually *is* no big deal. It's just something about me. Just like I told Mum. Completely unlike the way Matt saw it.

'I loved laughing with you outside Mr Trench's office,' Drew continues, 'but when I asked you about yourself, you hardly ever gave me a serious answer. And you rarely asked anything about me, either. You just keep things all jokey, on the surface . . .' He sighs.

'And even when . . . you know . . . we got together.' He swallows hard and stares into the Adventure Tree. 'You said you were going out with Matt. And then you weren't, but it was still *complicated*. It wasn't like you ever really liked me. You were just playing with me. I shouldn't have been surprised when you ran off last night.'

'But I *do* like you! I ran off because I thought you were trying to fix me up with your Deaf friend!'

His eyes flash. 'That's ridiculous and you know it.' Then he searches my face. 'Don't you?'

I hold his gaze. 'I do now.'

Drew looks down and then, balling his fists as if he's bracing himself, he makes eye contact with me again. 'Lex, look, I'm sorry if that's what you thought. I was genuinely trying to help and I didn't mean it to come across like that.' He takes a deep breath. 'But I wanted to find you today to tell you that I'm not interested in playing all these games. I've had a fantastic week with . . . some of the things that have happened. But I've also never felt more confused in my life. And I've had a pretty confusing life. I . . . I don't think I can do this. With you. So . . .' He turns away.

I catch him before he can leave. 'Why have you had a confusing life?'

He turns back, his eyes narrow. 'Are you asking me now because I just said you never asked about me?'

271

'No.'

He keeps looking at me.

'OK, maybe. But I do want to know. I really do. I want to know everything about you. I'm sorry about this week, it's been . . . strange.'

A tiny smile plays on Drew's lips at last. 'Tell me about it.'

'Tell me about *you* first.' I hold out my hand. 'In the leaves?'

Drew hesitates. Then he takes my hand. 'I'm going to regret this,' he says.

'I'm not.'

I smile and he – finally – smiles back properly.

We sit in our film set and Drew tells me things about his life and his parents and his brothers and sisters, who he misses, and more about his friends from back home. He tells me about how lost he felt in our school when he started because everyone knew everyone and no one talked to him and the only person he knew was Jess, and that wasn't much use. He says he was almost relieved to be Special Needs for the first time in his life because college was OK, plus it was such a relief to sit and laugh with me outside Mr Trench's office.

So then I realize what I've never asked him. What I just incorrectly assumed even though it drives me mad when people incorrectly assume stuff about me.

'Why are you an Improver, then,' I ask, 'if you're not a Non-Attender?'

He gives me a long look. 'Which was the one you were sure was your oh-so-exclusive category – because you're the only person in the world who's ever had some kind of difficulty at school?'

Never! 'Are you kidding? You're an Improver of the Third Kind? I don't believe you.'

'Probably because your category doesn't exist. I told you when you first mentioned it, Lex. Some people just learn differently. You're one of them. So am I.'

I laugh. 'Oh my God, no wonder Mr Trench was beside himself with delight! He didn't just put two Improvers together – he put two *thickies* together! And we produced his favourite bit of film!'

'See, you shouldn't say that. You shouldn't even *think* it. I'm serious, Lex.'

'OK, OK, I'm starting to get it. So what's your poison? Why are you a Type Three Improver?'

He hesitates. 'I'm severely dyslexic. My old school tried hard with me, but I still failed nearly all my Standard Grades – they're like the Scottish equivalent of GCSEs. That's why I'm doing some courses at the college, because Mr Trench has me taking a mixture of stuff now.'

'Severely dyslexic?' I frown. 'That sounds . . . severe.'

'It is. I have real trouble organizing things. I get my

thoughts in the wrong order, I get lost easily – that sort of thing. School has always been a problem for me. So yeah, I've been the other two types of Improver too, if I'm honest. I skipped school, I got into trouble. I felt like no one understood.'

I give him a lingering look. 'So you *are* a bad boy! I knew it.'

'Yup.' He nods seriously. 'If it means you'll look at me like that again, then I'm the *worst*.'

I think a minute. 'Is that why you have a special phone?'

Drew groans. 'God, Lex, don't you hate that word? *Special?*'

Oh wow, how did I actually manage to find someone who understands this stuff? 'Not really, special boy. Is that why you have a *weird and freaky, abnormal* phone?'

He grins. 'It's just a PDA – a palmtop computer. It helps because I can easily adjust the background colour and contrast, among other things.'

'So if you're dyslexic, does it mean you can't send text messages?'

'Lex, are you being deliberately . . . you know. You saw me text Aunt Sarah and Jess the other day. I might get my words and spellings muddled sometimes, but I'm exactly like everyone else, really.'

I poke him in the ribs, which I intend as playful except that it takes me a while to pull my hand away. I just love the feel of him.

'You're nothing like anyone else. And I'm not being deliberately . . . you know. Unless by "you know" you mean that I'm trying to get you to send me a text so that I have your number and I can text you all day when I'm supposed to be concentrating on other things that I struggle to concentrate on because lip-reading can be hard work.'

I collapse on the ground with the weight of that sentence.

'And breathe.' Drew laughs, taking his PDA out of his jacket pocket and then letting himself fall beside me. He holds it in the air above our heads. 'Tell me your number.'

Thirty seconds later my phone vibrates and I wriggle it out of the pocket of my jeans. The message reads: xxx

Drew's watching me and his eyebrows are dancing.

'So are those letters in the wrong order?' I ask.

'In the immortal words of Lex Murphy' – he gives me a stern look – '*Whatever. Shut up.*'

'I can't believe you just quoted me back at me!'

His eyes spark wickedly. 'Also, it's complicated and I'm going out with someone else and it's serious.' He doesn't stop there, either. He repeats what I shouted at him last night. Then he adds, 'But I'm still going to drive you crazy by kissing you in the hottest possible way and then dumping you. I'm Lex Murphy!'

I go to hit him but end up feeling up his shoulder

muscles instead. 'Whatever. Shut up. Look, it's not supposed to be easy. You've seen our film.'

Drew nods. 'I've *filmed* our film.'

'So you know it's all about the heartache and pain.' I let go and roll in the leaves, throwing some at him.

He throws more back. 'You're not kidding.'

I shrug into the autumn colours. 'That's just how it goes. Kiss, date, love, hate. *The Stages of Love.* In any order.'

He rolls right next to me, his face inches from mine. 'How about we stick to the first three?'

He covers me with his gorgeous body and makes my breath come out in delicious gasps. Then he props himself up on one elbow, pushes my hair out of my face and fans it carefully all around me until I can't take it any more and I reach up and find his lips with mine, pulling him down towards me.

We set the romantic leaves on fire until the end of lunch break.

The Bijou Cinema is pleased to announce the following new regular events:

Student Night Thursday

Special screenings for students aged 15+, featuring cult films, sometimes accompanied by Jess Hartford's interpretive dance. Audience participation encouraged. There will also be occasional screenings of short films from the local school film club, led by Lex Murphy and Drew Ashton. This follows the sell-out screening of the trail-blazing short film by the pioneer half-term Digital Media group, led by high-school teachers Stuart Trench and Natalie Cosgrove. Special commendation given to Lex Murphy and Drew Ashton's section: *The Stages of Love*.

Silver Screen Sunday

Special screenings for persons aged 55+, led by local

students Drew Ashton and Jess Hartford in conjunction with Hartford Residential Care, with films introduced by Lex Murphy, and tea and biscuits served by George Richards and Kathryn Ellison.

Mike Dell, owner and manager of the Bijou Cinema, says, 'We're pleased to cater for both ends of the audience spectrum here at the Bijou. In addition, these initiatives have brought a much-needed increase in foot-fall to our cinema and we are now able to remain open for business for the foreseeable future. I'd really like to thank our loyal regulars, George and Lex, and that new guy, Drew, for helping to make this possible.'

EXTREME KISSING

By Luisa Plaja

Two best friends. One extreme adventure.
Too many secrets…

Bethany is the sensible one with a long-term boyfriend, Carlota is the rebellious one with the wild past. All is fine in their world – except Carlota hates her stepdad and longs for her ex. And Bethany is worried that her boyfriend is about to dump her – and she's 'late'…

Carlota has a plan to put their troubles behind them on a crazy day out in London. She uses her favourite magazine to guide them on a life-changing adventure – setting real challenges from the glossy pages that lead to exclusive shopping, exciting snogging and … explosive secrets.

The magazine will take them everywhere they need to go – but will it make them reveal the truths they are keeping from each other?

SPLIT BY A KISS

By Luisa Plaja

I'm two different people. Literally. I'm split.

Jo has never been one of the popular kids . . .
until she moves to the USA. Suddenly the
coolest girls at her new high school adopt her,
and the hottest boy, Jake Matthews, notices her.
But when Jake picks her as his partner in the
kissing game Seven Minutes in Heaven, it's
not half as heavenly as she imagined!

Jo has a choice: should she carry on with Jake
for guaranteed popularity – or should she
tell him where to get off and risk losing
her new friends . . . ?

At this moment, Jo splits. She's Josie the Cool –
girlfriend of Jake, member of the in-crowd.
But she's also Jo the Nerd – rejected by the
It girls, single . . . ordinary. Will her two halves
ever come together again?

'A cute, sweet and funny read. Fans of
Louise Rennison will love it.'
Meg Cabot

SWAPPED BY A KISS

By Luisa Plaja

Rachel hates her life.

When on/off boyfriend David goes to a music festival she decides to surprise him – but she gets a shock of her own. Not only does she find David kissing someone else, but it's their friend Jo! Super-lovely, super-loved, all-round-perfect *Jo*.

Rachel runs away, wishing she could leave her life behind – and she suddenly finds herself in Jo's body! Can she keep this swap a secret? Can she unravel what's really going on? Can she get to grips with Jo's out-of-control curly hair?

And if she discovers that being in someone else's shoes isn't all it's cracked up to be, can she ever be herself again?